THE GIRL,
THE APPRENTICE,
AND THE DOGS OF IRON

THE RHIANNA CHRONICLES

THE GIRL, THE APPRENTICE, AND THE DOGS OF IRON

Book Two of The Rhianna Chronicles

Dave Luckett

SCHOLASTIC INC.

New York   Sydney
Mexico   enos Aires

No part of this publication may be reproduced in whole or in part, or stored in a retrieval system, or transmitted in any form or by any means, electronic, mechanical, photocopying, recording, or otherwise, without written permission of the publisher. For information regarding permission, write to Permissions Department, Scholastic Australia, P.O. Box 579, Lindfield, New South Wales, Australia 2070.

ISBN 0-439-41188-2

Text copyright © 2002 by Dave Luckett.

Originally published in Australia in 2002 by Omnibus Books under the title *Rhianna and the Dogs of Iron*.
All rights reserved. Published by Scholastic Inc., 557 Broadway, New York, NY 10012, by arrangement with Omnibus Books, an imprint of Scholastic Australia.

SCHOLASTIC and associated logos are trademarks and/or registered trademarks of Scholastic Inc.

12 11 10 9 8 7 6 5 4 3   5 6 7 8 9/0
                                              40

Printed in the U.S.A.
First American edition, February 2004

To Penny, Dyan, and Celia,
who always think I can do better,
and who are invariably right.

CHAPTER 1

The Clumsy Ones believed that the night was quiet, thought Eriseth. They were wrong, of course. In truth, the dark was full of sound. Every tree whispered in its own special voice. The oaks creaked in the chill night breeze, their bare twigs slithering gently over one another, and sounding quite different from the dry *tap-tap* of the alders, or the muted sigh of the willows, or the low rush of the wind in the elms, like distant water.

There were animal noises, too, scurryings and stealthy movements in the leaf litter on the forest floor. Even the flight of the owl could be heard, the almost silent bird that her people called *avanissa* — that is, darkhunter. It could only be heard if you had the ears to hear it, of course.

Eriseth could hear snowflakes falling; she could hear the field mice twitching in their winter sleep among the roots of the thicket where she crouched. The first houses of the village were a good four hundred paces away down the slope, but she heard the animals that the Clumsy Ones kept: the sleepy clucking of fowls, the bleating of sheep in the folds. Beyond, where the sloping land funneled down the valley to meet a dark line that cut off the winter stars, she could hear the drop and wash of the sea.

Eriseth gripped her bow a little tighter. She was frightened, she realized. She told herself that it was silly, that the forest was the same here as in her Home Grove. Still the feeling stayed. Something was watching her. She shook herself. Nonsense. It was just the open ground.

The trees of this last patch of woods ended here, a sudden stop as though a line had been drawn across the hill. Beyond were the cleared and plowed fields of the Clumsy Ones. They lay bare under the cold moon, frost riming the furrows. The forest that was Eriseth's home — her protector, and the provider for her people — was behind her, a hundred leagues of trees in numbers beyond counting. Eriseth's people, the Eldra, knew them all.

And now she had to leave the trees behind. Never before had she been out of their shelter. She had made this last stage of her journey at night, crossing the outlying fields and pastures with caution, and now she studied the open ground before her uneasily. Open ground, all bare beneath the stars, was exposed and dangerous. The Eldra avoided such places — for land which did not support trees did not support the Eldra, either.

But there was no choice now. Eriseth had come to the village of the Clumsy Ones alone, with a letter to deliver to a person she had never seen. The letter was a square of squirrel parchment, the writing burned in with a glowing needle, the square folded and sealed with beeswax. She touched her fingers to it where it was tucked safely under her left arm. The name on the parchment was one she had never heard before, but it was a good name, a noble name — *Serenir*. The Pole Star, as the Clumsy Ones would call it. The letter was for him. He was a magic worker.

He, thought Eriseth, in wonder. A magic worker, and a man. Arwenna, the Wisewoman who had written the letter, had told her that men worked magic, among the Clumsy Ones. Among the Eldra only women had magic, and they did not *work* it. It was part of them. You might as well say that they worked at breathing, or at standing up, or at singing. People who had to work at something couldn't be much good at it, thought Eriseth.

She sighed. Well, *she* wasn't. She had no magic at all, it seemed. The Clumsy Ones were her last chance. She might learn their ways. Their work.

The Clumsy Ones were great workers. Eriseth looked

down the moonlit slope at the open fields they had made from the forest. She disliked the sight. The Eldra never felled a tree. The forest was their home — it would be like hacking down their own doorposts. But the Clumsy Ones cleared the forest, plowed the ground and planted crops. Eriseth shuddered. The Clumsy Ones could work, all right, but they made of the earth a thing to be used, with iron axes to scrape it bare and iron plowshares to scar it, so it might grow the captive crops that were their food.

And Eriseth had to go to them. She glanced upwards at the moon and knew that dawn was not far off. Sighing, she started down the slope towards the houses, slinging her bow over her shoulder.

She had gone into the waning moonlight, her small figure smaller still with distance, when another hooded shadow parted from the darkness under the trees. It watched her, peering about, uneasy, just as she had been. Like part of the darkness it waited, and then it followed her, silent as smoke, down the slope towards the village. Even the dogs heard nothing, and it was as if the starlight flowed around and missed it.

On winter mornings, Loys Wildwood rose before the sun to fire up his forge. It would need to burn for an hour before it was fit to work iron, and the daylight would be short and gray. He had to make use of such hours of light as he had. Normally, the fire would be a job for an apprentice, not the master smith, but Loys had no apprentice. And, in truth, he enjoyed this hour before the rising of the sun: the bite of the crisp, cold air and the slow warming of the forge in the red glow.

He was working the bellows, watching the play of the flames, and thinking of the day's work. Rough iron billets were stacked by the wall, delivered yesterday from the ship that was still tied up to the pier at the bottom of the single village street. It might be best to begin the day by working some of the billets into bar iron. Then there were tools to be reforged. Already farmers were bringing in their spades and hoes to be repaired, ready for the work of ditching that would be needed with the thaw. Spring was not far away. Soon he would be making plowshares for the spring plowing . . .

The door creaked.

Loys knew at once that it was no farmer, no trader. No fisher, either. Those people rose early, but their footsteps were clear and open, careless. This caller's feet made no sound he could hear. In this last hour of the night, it was sometimes best not to question the folk that went abroad, and Loys knew that. He was no worker of magic himself, for he had no talent in that direction and his trade was with cold iron, but he knew what magic was.

"Welcome," he said, not turning around. "A cold morning. Warm yourself at my fire."

Now, there is magic and there is magic. Loys knew no spells, no chants, no runes or powers or charms. But was it by accident that he had used the polite greeting that the Eldra used themselves, between hunters chancemet in the forest?

Still there were no footsteps, and the waft of his visitor's passage was slight, so little that it could not be heard under the huff of the bellows. But there was a dark movement at the limit of his sight where the bench ran along the wall, and Loys turned his head away, again polite by the measure of the Eldra, not to look directly at his visitor.

Nor does one question a guest. Loys raked his fire into a mound of glowing charcoal and placed a pannikin of water on it. A cup of tansy tea would give heart to the raw morning. Only when it was made, the fragrant steam scenting the warm firelight of the forge, did he turn to offer it.

He was a man of easy ways, Loys Wildwood, the smith of Smallhaven, and gentle, for all his size and strength. One way and another, he had seen much in his life already. So in the first place he recognized his caller's kind, and in the second place he did not start and look uneasy. He offered the tea, speaking gently, and was not surprised that it was at first politely refused and then gratefully accepted, for this, too, was courtesy.

You might have taken her, perhaps, for a small girl in a hooded cape, gray-green goatswool as it had come from the fleece. Indeed, she *was* young for the Eldra — about the same as a ten-year-old among the Clumsy Ones, though she might have had many more years than that. The Eldra lived long lives, those of them that saw out their span.

And she was small. The Eldra could grow tall, and perhaps she would yet, but they were fine of bone and spare of body, with eyes large in a sharp face and ears that came to long, delicate points. Her hair was dark honey color, cropped around her face, but picking up coppery lights from the glowing forge.

Loys glanced at the doorway, and there, as he had expected, her bow was leaning. It was a tall, straight ash staff, straight because it was unstrung. This was a courtesy, too, not to bring a weapon into the house, a sign of trust. He sipped his tea gravely and said nothing, for it is not polite to ask a guest her business until she speaks of it herself.

She sipped her tea and set it aside, and then reached into her tunic, under the cape. A crackling, and she had brought out a letter, a sheet of parchment folded corners-to-center and sealed with wax. She put it into his hands, and Loys turned it over. He could read, but the name, written plain on the fold, meant nothing to him: *Serenir*. He frowned.

"I know nobody of this name, Lady," he said. He half expected that she would not reply, for few among the Eldra spoke the Hard Tongue, but she tilted her head and answered him.

"It is the same as the Pole Star, in your speech. He is a great maker of magic. A wizard." Her accent was like a bell, open, clear, but with a ring and a rhythm of its own.

He considered. "Pole Star? The North Star, that the Watchers guard and the Dog points out?"

She nodded. "The Hunters and the Hound, yes."

"Then I do know him. His name — at least, the name *we* call him — is Northstar, Antheus Northstar. And you have come to the right place, for he is a guest in my house. Also a guest in my house."

She cocked her head, appreciating the last, and then looked around. "Is he here now?" she asked, after a pause.

Loys hid a smile. "He is at my house, and still abed, I think. This is my forge, my place of work."

Her wide eyes widened farther. It was strange to one of the Eldra to be within a building at all. Stranger yet to be told that a man might have more than one building, for more than one purpose.

Loys banked his fire and fed it with more charcoal, to

burn evenly while he was away. He handed the letter back to her. "If you will follow, I will take you to him," he said.

She followed. And a shadow followed them both.

Meg Wildwood was surprised to see her husband back so soon from the forge, and more surprised still when he ushered in another guest. She was just having breakfast herself with her daughter, Rhianna, and Rhianna's Master, the Magister Antheus Northstar. Loys had been wrong to think that the Magister would still be asleep. Still, you would think that the Mage on the Queen's Council was far too important a person to be sitting in the kitchen of a village smith, or to be eating ordinary oat porridge for breakfast, no matter how clean and comfortable the kitchen, or good the porridge. But Magister Northstar never gave himself airs. He was deep in discussion with his apprentice as the smith entered.

". . . Yes, indeed, the new moon is certainly the best time for casting water spells, but I believe that is because it's the time of the spring tide, the greatest height of the waters, not simply the phase of the moon . . . eh?"

Rhianna was looking straight past him. He swung around, saw who was entering, and stood politely. He was only a small man, and he wasn't wearing his tall wizard's hat inside the house, so he looked rather ordinary, despite his robe with the stars and his long white beard.

At least, he looked rather ordinary until you saw his eyes, faded blue like an autumn sky, and as deep.

Rhianna stood, too, a girl ten or eleven years old, brown-haired, with a freckled nose. Her book lay open on the table with a drawing on the uppermost page, a careful sketch of an icicle, showing how it broke sunlight into colors. Rhianna was studying magic, but in her own way, the way of the Wild Magic — that is, the magic that comes straight from the land and the water — and not as Mages learned it, with word and charm. She put her hand to her throat, where a rich jewel sparkled, a jewel that was far out of place on a village girl. It was rubies and gold, a piece to grace a princess.

Eriseth saw it, and wondered.

She had pushed back the hood of her cloak on entering the warm kitchen. Now she looked around her, at the hearth with its pothooks and iron grate, at the bread-oven beside it, the mantelshelf with its candlesticks, the sideboard for linen and the best china, and the solid oak table. She nodded, suddenly shy and wary of these large people with their booming voices.

Loys looked down at her. "Welcome to my house," he said, formal as a host should be, and she glanced up.

"*Hethoorch yrn' ty*," she whispered.

"And peace be with you, too, forest-child," said Magister Northstar. "You have come far, I think."

Her words in reply were stilted, a rehearsed speech. "From Arwenna, whom you know, Serenir," she said. "She greets you and bids me give you this." She held out the letter.

He took it, and held it briefly before he broke the seal and unfolded it. A glance under his white brows at the bearer, and then he read. The others stood awkwardly, Rhianna inspecting the Eldran girl, her parents regarding each other and the Magister as he spelled carefully through the letter, turned back to the top and read it again. Then he looked up, folding the parchment carefully.

"Arwenna gave you no other message?" he asked.

"No, Serenir. Only that she greets you in old friendship."

He smiled, but it was a smile both brief and slight. "Old friendship. Yes, indeed. You know what Arwenna has written, Eriseth?" She nodded. "So you should. It concerns you. Arwenna asks much." She nodded again. He frowned, and looked down at the letter. "But not more than she is owed. Strange that this comes to me here and now." He tapped his chin with the folded parchment. Then he turned to the blacksmith. "Loys, you have no apprentice at present, I think?"

Loys Wildwood blinked, a little confused by the sharp turn in the conversation. He glanced at his wife, and then answered: "No, Magister. None of the village boys seems to want to learn the forge, all hot and sweaty as it is. It's all farming, hereabouts, and all of them will have land or their own father's trade to inherit." He looked at Meg again, and smiled gently, in a way that said *It's not your fault, love*, as he went on: "I have no son of my own, and Rhianna — well, her Wild Magic would never do, working cold iron."

Magister Northstar nodded. "Then I have a favor to ask. Here is Eriseth. Her Birth Grove was Arwenna's, so her name after our custom would be Eriseth Arwensgrove. There are reasons why she cannot practice magic in the way of the Eldra. Arwenna, her Wisewoman, has therefore sent her to us, with a request that she learn the craft of iron, so that she can take it back to her people."

He bowed his head, as if contemplating. "There is a strangeness about this. The Eldra are owed it, for the peace of the border that they have kept these many years. Yet they might have wished for many other things I could not grant. Here, I have the means ready to my hand, if you will consent. The Queen's Council will pay you the usual apprenticeship fee. From what Arwenna has written, Eriseth has already done what work in iron she can among the Eldra. Her arrowheads are her own work, Arwenna says, and they are iron. The Eldra usually use finely chipped stone."

Loys Wildwood's brows rose. "Let me see," he said,

and silently the Eldra girl drew a long arrow from the quiver at her waist. The pointed head, Rhianna could see, was iron, dimpled and with rust around the edges.

"Ah," said Loys, running a finger over it. "You needed to quench this with hot oil to keep it from rust. And why did you use a round-face hammer? You needed a flat-face for the edges, at least, and a file . . ."

"Master, I used a stone on another stone, pounding it out from a piece of iron that fell from the sky. It was only a small piece, enough for five arrowheads. But I did all I could, and found out how little I know. I would like to know more, if you will teach me."

Loys frowned. "Well . . . I do need an apprentice. But the forge is hard, heavy work. Do you think . . . ?" He made a small gesture at Eriseth, slight and lightboned as she was.

Magister Northstar stirred. "On that score, I think you need have no fears. The Eldra are fine made, no doubt, but their bodies are strong and enduring. Eriseth's bow pulls far more than she weighs, but she could shoot it all day, if she needed to. I'll warrant she can do the work, if she wills."

Loys looked across at his wife. Meg smiled, as if to say *It's up to you*. He turned to Eriseth. "She must say it herself, then. Eriseth, I am willing to bind you as apprentice. I am to find your board and lodging and keep, and I am to teach you the trade of iron. You are to work in the forge and obey me as you would your fath —" he caught the Magister's warning glance "— your Wisewoman. The bargain is on liking for three months, then may only be ended when we both will it, or at the end of seven years. You will be a smith yourself, then. Say now, are you willing to make this bargain?"

Eriseth did not smile. Her face was solemn and still. "I am willing, Master."

Loys held out his hand. She took it. The signing of the apprenticeship deed would come later, but everyone in that kitchen knew that the word had been given and the bargain sealed then and there.

Rhianna stood frowning. She didn't know this person, Eriseth. It had all happened too quickly.

The silent listener outside the kitchen window frowned, too. Dawn was full abroad now, and there were people about in the village street. It was well that the house of the smith was on the slope above the village, but the Watcher had to leave. Soon there would be too much light — and dogs, with their keen noses, are not fooled by a don't-look-at-me spell. She moved away, and it was as if a faint shadow had passed over the grass of the meadows, a ripple of the morning breeze that drifted up towards the patch of woods that crowned the slope. Then it was among the trees and gone.

14

CHAPTER 2

"The colors are in the light, not the mist. The mist just shows them," remarked Rhianna to her Master.

"Mm? Oh. Yes. Perhaps."

Rhianna and Magister Northstar were sitting by the bank of a small stream, with the Wizard's staff leaning on a large, flat stone between them. The stream was the one that flowed through the village, but they had walked out beyond the houses, and then up the slope beside its banks. They had not spoken, and now had reached the hills, where the water cascaded over rocks and tumbled in a run of rapids, throwing up fine spray. The sun had come out for a while, and in that mild sunlight, the first hint of the coming spring, the spray was shot through with rainbows. That was what they had come to see. At least, that had been the idea, arranged the previous night, before Eriseth's arrival.

Not far upstream, in a cleft between the hills, the

forests loomed, bare and massive and gloomy, but sifting pale light in slanting shafts between the trees. Beyond them a line of distant mountains made a blue ragged line against the rim of the sky. Rhianna watched the rainbows above the stream, seeing how they came and went among the curtains of drifting mist thrown up by the rapids, but Magister Northstar was watching the light-shot army of the trees, and the far mountains.

Over towards those mountains was the land of the Eldra, and beyond them their forests continued until the land met the Western Sea. There in those far forests lay Arwensgrove, Eriseth's home. Like all the Groves, it was a green place among mighty oaks. The houses, built around the trunks of the trees, were of woven branches stopped with clay and covered with creepers. Their roof-beams were living tree limbs, their pillars the boles of the trees themselves. Strange houses for a strange people, buildings that were more than half alive.

Northstar sat, lost in thought, remembering. A very young wizard had once traveled to the Eldra lands as a junior assistant to an earlier Queen's Councillor. The Councillor was to sign a treaty in the Queen's Name, fixing a border between the lands of the Eldra and those of the Queen's People. There the young wizard had met an Eldra songsinger who was already marked as wise beyond her years.

Wise she was, for she had gently prevented a young fool from making a worse fool of himself. That was long ago, and even wizards were young once. Arwenna Song-singer. Arwenna the Wise, now. He wondered, as he had wondered many times before, if she had changed. Perhaps. But not as much as he. The Eldra lived long lives. That had been one of the several things that the young wizard had forgotten.

Rhianna watched him a moment, but he said no more. She considered the play of the rainbows, and a thought came: *These are such little rainbows, and close by. Where's the pot of gold, I wonder.* She turned her head to glance at Magister Northstar. He was still watching the trees, brows creased, eyes seeming to stare at something far away.

"I said, it's the misty spray that shows the rainbows, with the sun," she repeated, to have something to say. "I wonder if I could make more? Magister?"

He shook his head a little. "Oh, yes. Yes, indeed. I'm sure you could." He fell silent again, still staring towards the forest.

Rhianna smiled. It wasn't often that the Magister let her try a new working. The Wild Magic was slippery, hard to hold, hard to control. It wanted to do larger things all the time, and go its own way. Rhianna was learning to control it, but it was difficult.

Now she slipped her jewel off, over her head, so that she could use the Wild Magic.

The jewel she wore was magic, too, of a sort. Rhianna had to wear it, for it stopped the Wild Magic from rushing in. All magic comes from the land, the sea, the air around, from wind and fire, rain and sunshine. Rhianna's gift was so strong that she took up all the magic for the whole district, so that there was none for anyone else. Worse, the magic would run out of control unless she knew exactly what she was doing, and used no more than she absolutely had to. That was why she spent long hours drawing and studying anything she needed to work with, until she knew it so well that she could not make a mistake. For the Wild Magic was dangerous, too. There was no telling what it might do if it were not controlled.

Now, with the jewel off, Rhianna let the magic fill her, and it was like drinking sunshine. She felt her vision expand. Colors seemed to grow more brilliant, shapes seemed more defined and solid. The world became brighter, sharper, more alive.

She watched a rainbow in the spray. There were days when you could see two rainbows, one within another, and that was wonderful. Could she make the mist do that here?

The magic slipped out, a little flow of it, and misty tendrils rose from the stream, winding together, binding, building. The sun seemed to strengthen behind them, the mist brightened, and there they were: two rainbows, two colored arches like reflections of each other, with jeweled colors brighter than any paint, more gorgeous than any picture. Rhianna smiled again. Two was all very well, but she thought how wonderful *three* rainbows would be. Certainly such a thing would be more than that Eldra girl could do, the one that Father had taken on as apprentice.

No sooner thought than done. She built the mist up further until a wall of silvery vapor filled the whole dell, and then there were three rainbows, beautiful enough to make a person's mouth fall open.

Rhianna felt strong and sure in her power, and eager to try for something more striking yet, something to amaze Magister Northstar, something far better than Father's new apprentice could manage. Could the mist be made to braid the rainbows together, like ribbons of silk, if it moved about? Could the rainbows be made to flutter, to dance like ribbons swirled by a shake of the head? Could she make them move and weave like living things? Charmed by the glorious colors and the brightness of the rainbows, Rhianna thought that as a sort of whimsy. Anyone might daydream — but this was the Wild Magic, and daydreams are perilous things.

The surface of the little stream seemed to come to a

boil, and suddenly the mist was a great rolling cloud and the air became thick. The mist curdled into fog, still rushing up from the water like steam from a great boiling kettle, and the rainbows disappeared. The bank of vapor darkened and thickened still further, and out of the rolling solid bank came the grumble of thunder. The fog swirled and rolled, the rush of the stream was muffled, and the air became still, treacly, and cold.

Rhianna had just time enough to think, *No, that's not what I meant*, when the fog rolled over her and Magister Northstar, billowing and thickening as it went. The woods disappeared, and so did the stream and all other things in the world, suddenly blotted out behind a damp gray wall. Magister Northstar was within a hand's touch, yet Rhianna couldn't see him. There were just billows of gray fog, moving in gusts past her face. The world became the fog, a damp chill hand pressed over her face, a nothingness before her eyes.

Worse, in the fog she could hear things moving. Rhianna had no idea what sorts of things they might be, but she had asked for movement, for life, and she had gotten what she asked for. This was movement, this was life, like the life you see when you turn over a stone, for the things that moved in the fog were wet and cold. They croaked at her with frogs' voices, and with slurpings like the slimy walking of a snail, and there were half seen shapes that glowed green like rotten wood in the fog, vague unpleasing shapes like things that have been left too long out in the rain. She shrank away, her hand to her mouth. This was not what she had meant, not at all.

And then a shaft of silver light blazed out. There was a roar, and the cold little breeze became a driving wind. The fog rolled and billowed, heaving like a great wounded animal, and Rhianna sat stunned and helpless. At times like this, when the Wild Magic ran out of control, it was as if the Magic was using her, not the other way around.

The Magister's voice came, a strong rolling chant quite unlike his speaking voice. It was a chant of warmth and sunlight, of dry drowsy summer days, full of bee-buzz and gentle breezes. It was the opposite to everything that is dank and wet and cold, and the fog heard it. It thinned, losing by slow degrees its dark blank grayness, becoming a silvery mist. Little by little, the world returned. The stream could be heard again, splashing and rushing down the rocks, and the trees behind picked up the wind, too. It gave them their voices, rolling and roaring under the Magister's words like a choir singing a song with no words that Rhianna could understand. And still the fog rolled away down the valley, a solid bank of vapor, covering field and stream.

When the spray and mist from the waters were no

more than should have been there, Magister Northstar stopped his chant. His staff slipped down in his hand. Its butt thudded on the earth, and he leaned on it, hunching his shoulders, weary, watching the cloud roll down the valley.

The fog poured out like milk from a jug. It blanketed the village for a while, and then spread out over the sea. Magister Northstar watched it go, and his face was tight.

He turned towards Rhianna, frowning deeply. When he spoke, his voice was sharp with worry, slowly growing into anger. "That fog will reach the bay and blow out to sea, Rhianna, where I can do nothing about it. There are seafarers whose lives may be endangered by it. Not to mention the mist-seemings you summoned with it. Fortunately, they are only seemings, and will be gone with the fog. But there are much worse things that could have answered you. What on earth possessed you to do such a thing? Put that necklace back on at once!"

Rhianna did so. The magic was blown out like a candle, and just like blowing out a candle, it felt as though she was left in the dark. "You said I could try it . . ." she started.

Magister Northstar's eyes widened. "I?" he snapped. "I said no such thing. I said it could be done, not that you should try to do it. What were you thinking of, Rhianna?"

Rhianna felt her throat constrict. Honestly, she couldn't say what she had been thinking. Not enough about control, certainly, or about not using more of the Wild Magic than necessary. But what had she been thinking about instead?

Magister Northstar was shaking his head. "This must not happen again, Rhianna. You must not take the jewel off again. You hear me? You must not. Not until you have control."

Rhianna lowered her head, scowling. If she were to wait until she was certain of perfect control, she would never be able to use her magic at all.

"It's no use sulking, Rhianna." The Magister's voice was sharp and worried now. "The Wild Magic is still too powerful for you. If you start taking the jewel off whenever you want to, I shall have to further bespell it so that you can't remove it."

Rhianna slowly lifted her face to him. Her eyes were bright and angry. "I'm not sulking. You *did* say that I could try, only you weren't paying attention. You were looking at the forest and not listening. And do you really think that you could make me keep the jewel on, if I didn't want to?"

The Magister stared at her. Then, slowly, he nodded. "I . . . see. Yes." He cleared his throat. "Well, perhaps so.

I beg your pardon for not attending more closely. But you must keep it on, Rhianna. If you won't, it'll come down to a Wizard's Contest — and nobody wins those. Please. For everyone's sake, do as I ask."

Rhianna looked away, embarrassed. She nodded.

He tried to smile. "Good." He unbent carefully and hitched up his staff, speaking more briskly. "And now, if you have finished the drawing, we can go back."

"Already?" This would mean going back to school. Rhianna had counted on having the morning free.

"Yes. I must return to Avalon and the College. And the Council. The Western Islanders have been raiding again, and Hrothwil, who calls himself their King, must be given a sharp reminder. If he will not control his folk, his own lands must pay for it. We will raid him in return, and perhaps then he will listen when we speak." The Magister was the Chancellor of Wizardly College and the Mage on the Queen's Council. Rhianna tried to remember that he had other things to do besides tutor her. Indeed, he did look worried.

"Why do they raid, Magister? How have we annoyed them?"

He made an impatient gesture. "We annoy them by living in peace and by having things they want. And they raid because there is renown in fighting. Warriors are honored among them, but a warrior without a fight is a useless thing. One day they might learn that it is better to do without either. I hope so. But that's not your problem. Your problem is controlling your magic. Remember, Rhianna, exactness. Know exactly what you want to do and use as little magic as possible. And keep that jewel on. I have your promise, mind."

Yes, thought Rhianna, drearily. *You have my promise. But not forever.*

They walked back to the village, Rhianna dawdling behind.

The Eldra do not use rods or runes in their magic, nor anything heavy or easy to break, for they must carry with them all that they own. They use no crystal balls to talk at a distance. Thus the Watcher stared into a pool of water between the roots of a great oak, and another face looked out of it.

"It is as we feared," the Watcher said. She spoke in the Eldra tongue, low and liquid, like an echo of the rush of water or the wind in the trees. "Arwenna has sent Eriseth, who has no magic, to learn the craft of the Clumsy Ones. The craft of iron."

The face in the pool was that of Merched the Wise-woman. She was in her Grove across the mountains, watching a pool of her own. Her face hardened in the shifting light on the water. "Iron," she spat. "What sort of thing is that for a daughter of the trees to learn? What is it for? To make axes that will fell the forest?"

"To make arrowheads that will fell our people, more likely. Arwenna was always one to rule."

"Arwenna. *Wisewoman*." The last word was a bitter curse. "So *wise* is Arwenna that she would destroy all that we are. I said it was a mistake, allowing the Clumsy Ones any land at all. We should have banded together, all the Groves, to drive them out. But *wise* Arwenna said that we could learn from each other. Learn! Now we see the learning she would have from the Clumsy Ones. Greed and iron, and Arwenna ruling over us all."

The Watcher who had followed Eriseth did not reply at once. Pale sunlight filtered through the trees, but tall clouds were massing over the sea. The air felt thick and cold. *Snow soon, perhaps*, she thought. She drew her goatswool cloak about her for warmth, and strength from the Grove for her magic. It was better here than down among the fields of the Clumsy Ones, all open to the sky as they were, but this small stand of trees was too little, and too confined, for one of the Eldra.

"We can do little for now but watch," said Merched's face in the water. "We cannot strike at Eriseth ourselves, for if we were found out, it would ruin us. Arwenna would destroy us. But she will make a mistake. Let Eriseth forge an axe-head, or a plow-blade . . ."

"And if she does not?"

Merched's eyes glittered in the shifting pool. It might have been the ripple of clouds crossing the sky. "Then we must use other means. Kaldi's ship will dock in the harbor at Smallhaven in a day or so. He will act as a merchant. Once aboard a Western Isles ship, Eriseth could be taken anywhere, and no blame to us. After all, who can say what the Clumsy Ones from the Western Isles would do? They and the Easterners — the Queen's People — are always raiding and fighting each other. Indeed, if they took Eriseth, it would make Arwenna look bad, for she is the one saying that we must tie ourselves more closely to the Clumsy Ones." She considered. "You have done well. Can you watch them, still?"

"Only by night. The Clumsy Ones could not see a pig in a porridge bowl, but their dogs are not so dull. Yet what I can do should be enough."

"Very well. Watch, and tell me as soon as you have seen. Perhaps we shall have a surprise yet for Arwenna, with her peace and tenderness for the Clumsy Ones. She may find that she is not the only one who can wield iron to her profit," Merched's mouth snapped shut.

The Watcher's eyes narrowed, as she wondered what Merched meant by that. But Merched went on: "So now.

Hunt, then rest. In two days I will be here, listening for you, as dawn comes up. Farewell."

The face in the pool rippled and was gone, and the Watcher found herself watching her own reflection. She straightened. She was hungry, but dried meat and flat-bread must do for today. Perhaps she would pick up a rabbit or a rook or two when dusk began to fall.

She ate her provisions and rolled herself in her cloak. The day crept on, becoming grayer. Snow began to filter down about noon, but by then she was fast asleep.

Days passed. Magister Northstar returned to Avalon, to his College and the Queen's Council and affairs of State. Determined to impress him, Rhianna was working hard at controlling her magic. She realized that the colors she had seen through the icicle and in the mist could also be seen when sunlight shone through a drop of water hanging from the window outside her room.

One afternoon she was doing the drawing again, for she had seen that the colors in the droplet were exactly the same as the colors of the rainbow. The paints in her paintbox didn't do them full justice. It was growing dark now, though, and the colors were gone.

The front door opened and closed. Rhianna heard her mother's voice, and then a murmur. Someone else was speaking. Her father must be home from the forge. She wiped her hands on a rag and picked up the drawing to show it to him — she was pleased with it, and was sure he would be, too. She went to the door of the kitchen.

Her father was still warm and ruddy from the forge, though the weather outside was cold and blustery. He shed warmth and good cheer in about equal amounts, standing with his back to Rhianna at the sluice, pumping up cold water to wash in. That meant he was finished for the day. There was still light in the sky, so it was early for him.

As he scrubbed his neck, Meg was saying, "Done at the forge already, dear?"

Loys spluttered and emerged from the basin. He picked up the soap and began on his face. "Yes. We finished that stack of tools — by halfway through it Eriseth was able to do the pumping and turning herself, and I only needed to do the striking. She had the color just right, never too hot. Then I taught her the annealing. She was quick at that, too. Never a complaint out of her, either, though you know how hard and dirty that job is."

Rhianna opened her mouth. She was about to tell her father about her drawing and the discovery she had made about rainbows in drops of rain, when the door opened again and in came Eriseth.

She too was red from the fire of the forge, and her face was sooty. There was a smear of black on her brow where she had wiped her hand across it. She stood uncertainly on the step, but Loys gestured her in.

"'Lo, Eris. Finished that last stand?"

Eriseth grinned, a sudden flash of light in her blackened face. "Yes, Master. The oil's nearly gone, though."

Loys nodded. "Aye. I thought it would be. Get some more tomorrow." As the Eldra girl still stood in the doorway, he added, "Come in, come in. Soap and water here — you'll need to clean up for supper. You'll be ready to eat, I should think. You did a lot of work today."

Rhianna lifted her drawing to show it. "Father, look . . ." she started.

"And it was good work, too," Loys went on. "Just one thing, Eris. You know when you were tempering the inside of those hoe blades? Well, you really need to reverse your grip on the tongs so the curve of the blade is towards you . . ."

Eriseth scrubbed her hands, nodding carefully. Loys continued on the subject of hoe blades until supper was laid, drawing invisible plans on the tabletop with a forefinger while Eriseth sat and listened, frowning with concentration. Rhianna was called to help set the table.

All through supper her father talked to his apprentice. Rhianna never did get the chance to show him her drawing and tell him what she had found out. All she could do was listen while he talked to Eriseth and praised her work.

Among the trees, the Watcher breathed on the surface of the pool, and the face of Merched the Wisewoman formed, as if it were her own reflection.

"Eriseth is taking to the craft of iron like a weasel to a rabbit," said the Watcher. "In a little while she will already have learned too much. We must stop her, or she will bring iron to the forest and we will lose it forever."

Merched frowned, then nodded. "I think you're right. Is Kaldi's ship there yet?"

"A new ship came in today, flying a black raven flag."

"That's him. The raven is his own sign. Go to him. He has been told to look for you in the nearest trees. A tall man, heavy, redheaded and redbearded, with a silver armband. He is a Western Islander, full of pride and mad for wealth and fame, like all of them. Tell him to take the girl. I will shout it out to the Council of Wisewomen, that the Clumsy Ones are not to be trusted."

The Watcher nodded, and the water of the pool rippled. The face of Merched was gone.

CHAPTER 3

Being ignored grew worse and worse. First Magister Northstar, then Father. Nobody wanted to listen to Rhianna. Nobody cared about *her* work, the work of learning to control the Wild Magic.

Another day had gone past. A whole day of listening to her father saying what a wonderful worker Eriseth was. To hear Father talk, she chewed iron bars and spat out perfect red-hot nails. Now he had gone out early, to help his apprentice.

Ha! If she's such a great worker, why does Father have to work longer hours himself?

Even Magister Northstar was behaving oddly. Rhianna had shown him her drawing by spellcaster, she in her kitchen at home, he in his study at Wizardly College across the water. The Magister had said it was very nice, and told her that he'd sent her a book about rainbows. But he had seemed absent and inattentive. He had asked after Eriseth with far more interest than he paid to Rhianna's careful work.

And the book he had promised had not arrived. Rhianna had been down to the pier to inquire if the ship that had just come in had brought a book for the daughter of the smith, but the sailor had simply shrugged his shoulders. The ship was a Western Isles craft. It had not come from Home Island, and it carried no book.

The disappointment had been the last straw.

Rhianna stamped angrily among the puddles, muttering to herself. It was cold, wet, and foggy, with all the people indoors, and she was wearing her gray-green oiled-wool cloak. Not that she really noticed the weather, for she was thinking about how unfair it all was. Nobody was interested in what she was doing. Nobody cared about her. Suddenly, tears were sliding down her face. Nobody thought her Wild Magic was any use, anyway. Well, they were right. It wasn't much.

I can't so much as mend a stocking with my magic unless I look at every single thread and know whether it was spun right or left-handed, thought Rhianna. *I almost have to know the name of the sheep whose wool it was spun from. What use is magic like that?*

The worst of it was that Father didn't seem to care about what she did. He was too interested in teaching Eriseth. It wasn't *fair*.

She passed between the houses and came to the stile at the head of the path that would take her home. But she didn't want to go home. She didn't want anyone to see her with her face all red and blotchy. Instead, she turned right and followed her ears to the stream, through the heavier fog that seemed to boil off its waters. Here she could sit on a damp stone, flip pebbles into the water, and think her own bitter thoughts. The forge was just down the street a little way, but Rhianna didn't want to hear or see any reminder at all of Eriseth.

The stream was high and running strongly in late winter spate. Rhianna found that her favorite spot was actually underwater. It was a sheltered place where alders leaned over the bank. In summer there was a shelf of pebbles here in a sort of little beach, but now the beach was covered with fast-running water, and the best she could do was to lean on the trunk and watch the current swirling past her feet.

Water. She watched the eddies and bubbles and ripples as the stream bounced down towards the sea, and around her the fog hung in thick folds like a curtain. There was nobody around, and she really couldn't stay for too long, for it was damp and cold here, but for a while she needed to be by herself.

She had been studying water for a long time now: falling rain and snow and ice, and fog like this, too — it was just water floating in the air. Surely she should know enough by now. She looked around and saw nothing but the curtain of mist, heard nothing but the voice of the stream. She reached up and pulled the jewel off her neck, over her head. She hung it on its chain over a twig, making sure it was secure.

As soon as it left her skin, the Wild Magic came flooding in from everywhere around her, filling her up. As before, it felt like plunging into cool, tingly water, but it also felt right. It felt as if this was the way she *should* be; that she was blinded and deafened by the jewel.

Now she looked about for something to do with the Wild Magic. Nobody thought it worth giving her credit for what she had learned. *Well*, she thought, *now we shall see. I'm so tired of people telling me I mustn't do things. Why can't I, when* she *can be as clever as she likes, and everyone cheers?*

The mist swirled. Rhianna thought about that. She remembered what she had done with the mist before, and how it had all gone wrong. Magister Northstar had rescued her. Her mouth took on a discontented twist.

He didn't have to do that. I could have managed. Why did he have to get involved, and then give me that lecture? Everything I do is fenced around. I'm not allowed to do anything. And it's not as though anything bad happened. All I did was thicken the mist, like this . . .

35

The curtains around her thickened. More and more fog billowed up from the stream, and the world disappeared into a blank gray wall, just as it had before. But this time it was only fog. Rhianna had controlled her use of the Wild Magic, and there were no slurpings and vague shadows. *See? I can manage it perfectly well, if I'm given a chance. Just as Eriseth Treeswinger, or whatever she calls herself, can manage iron . . .*

Suddenly, a hard hand clamped over her mouth, and another pulled the deep hood of her cloak over her head. Over her eyes, so that she couldn't see. She couldn't cry out, either. A heavily muscled arm lifted her as if she were a bundle of rags, and began to carry her away.

She tried to scream, and couldn't. The hand stayed locked on her mouth. The hood muffled her head. Panic gripped her. What was this? Who? She wriggled, and the arm tightened like an iron band, crushing the breath from her. She struggled, and the man didn't even grunt. He was far too strong.

He started to run, and she began to slide into helpless shock. Then he stopped suddenly. He stood a moment, and then he moved off in a different direction. Again he stopped, and turned slowly around, like someone trying to get his bearings. He said a word in a soft whisper, a single word that she didn't know.

The fog! It's confusing him. He can't see which way to go! But that means . . .

With that thought came another. Rhianna smothered her rising panic. She called up in her mind a picture of her place by the stream. She knew it well, summer and winter, and she knew fog and what came in fog. What *could* come in fog, what had come before when she called. *Mist-seemings*, Magister Northstar had called them. Nothing more than seemings. Things that seemed to be there.

She let out a little more of the Wild Magic. Her eyes, muffled in the hood, saw only darkness, but she knew there was swirling fog outside, deepening and thickening until a hand could not be seen in front of the face. Careful, desperate, she shaped the Wild Magic. She was blinded, and yet she knew what she wanted it to do. . . .

Out in the fog, something croaked. Something moved squishily, like a piece of tarpaper being pulled up, and thumped wetly on the ground. It gave a deep gulping sound, like a toad the size of a barrel catching a fly the size of a blackbird. And then it moved again, closer.

It chuckled and gurgled in the fog, and that was a fearful thing to hear. Rhianna could imagine it, though: slimy, unseen, moving wetly, something like a frog and something like a jelly. It would be squat and uncouth, like a toad, and it would glow, but dimly, with a sick pale light. It would have a wet wide mouth and eyes that were patches of cold green fire. Steel could not hurt it, any more than a knife could cut water. It moved in a series of lollops and ripples, like a snail, like a frog. And it was coming closer.

The man was shuffling backwards now, trying to get away.

That's no use, thought Rhianna. *There's another one behind you.*

He swung around and saw what she meant him to see, and he gave a cry. The arm around her loosened, and the hand on her mouth was gone for a moment as he groped at his side, perhaps reaching for a sword.

Rhianna seized her chance. A wriggle, and she was free of the arm. As soon as she had foot on ground, she ducked and ran for her life into the fog, pulling the hood away from her eyes as she did.

She ran, and the fog covered her. She spent a little more power to call it up again, and it settled like a deep gray blanket over the world. But she knew the ground she ran over. Here was the stone with the notch in it that was just before the wall to the Treesongs' back garden. She turned left, sharply. Twenty paces would bring her to the path that led to the street.

She looked back. Fog covered the world. She had never seen the man, never seen his face. In the blank grayness, perhaps he gazed out in fear, gripping a sword against things that seemed to be there. But she had no intention of letting the fog break up now. Let him stare into it, biting his lips and fearing.

Here was the street. Only a hundred paces away was the smithy, where her father was at work. And Eriseth. But Rhianna had no mind for that. She ran like a deer down the fog-shrouded street, to where the welcome glow of her father's forge showed through the mist.

"Father! Father, help!" she called. And rushed into the warm smithy like a blast of cold wind, into her father's arms and his instant concern.

She told her story in gulps. Halfway through, Loys caught up his heavy hammer and strode to the front of the forge. Fog still rolled down the street, towards the sea. He frowned. "Can you stop it?" he asked, urgently. "We'll never find him in this."

Rhianna nodded, a little doubtfully. The Wild Magic was easier to start than to stop, and she had not done this before. But she began the counter-magic, thinking of summer days and sunny meadows, and the cold dampness of the fog began to lift a little. And the fog-things, too. They were made of the fog itself, really, and would be gone with it, as her Master had said. Suddenly, she did not want her father to see what she had done. She concentrated on making the fog lift.

Loys watched it. "Good," he said. "You're all right, Rhianna? No hurts?" She shook her head. He watched her narrowly, and then nodded. "I'll raise the neighbors, then. You keep on thinning the fog. Eris, you have your bow?"

"Yes, Master." Eriseth caught it up from where it leaned against the wall. She braced it against the ground, pulled its top down with one hand while bending it by leaning into it with her knee. The loop of the string slid into place, and the bow was strung and ready for use.

Loys looked out again. Already there was a hint of sun. "Good. Stay here. Eris, guard her." He went to the open front of the smithy and his great chest filled out. "Hue and cry!" he shouted. "Up, up, neighbors, to me, to me!" And he plunged into the fog, still calling.

Doors opened along the street. People came to their shopfronts. Mr. Weaver from his loom, Mr. Tines the tinker, Mr. Cartmell from his ropewalk, the Mallet brothers from their chandler's shop. The hue and cry had been raised. They knew what to do. They snatched up weapons or tools and they followed the smith.

Rhianna and Eriseth were left to stare at one another. After a while, Rhianna found that she was shaking. Determined not to let the Eldra girl see it, she scowled and stared at the floor, saying nothing, still working at the unsummoning, until her mother came running in, called by the commotion.

And then she was gathered up into her mother's arms, and was soothed and comforted until she stopped shaking, while Eriseth watched, expressionless.

"There's nobody there now, Rhianna. But you left this," said Loys Wildwood. He held up the pendant, and Rhianna's mouth dropped open.

He nodded grimly. "You shouldn't have taken it off, Rhianna. We will talk of this later. Now, tell me again. You say you never saw the fellow?"

And so she had to tell it all again. Her father and her mother and her neighbors listened and looked at one another.

"It wasn't one of us," said Mr. Cartmell. "Nobody from Smallhaven would do such a thing." He seemed very sure of it.

Loys frowned. "We hope." He stroked his chin. "But whoever it was, he was confused in the fog. That might mean that he was a stranger to Smallhaven, although anyone could get lost in this. But there *are* strangers in port, and a man might find his way back to the harbor, even in a fog, simply by following the stream." He made up his mind. "We should question them. Rhianna, you come, too. You might recognize something." He swung around and walked down the street, towards the sea.

The ship at the pier was a Western Islander, long and

lean, with decks only at the fore and aft where the helmsman stood, and a deep waist for cargo. A few sailors sat or stood about, working on gear, and a tall redbearded man stood by the tiller, thumbs in belt, watching the tendrils of fog sweeping out over the water.

He turned as the villagers came in sight. There were ten or fifteen people behind Rhianna and Loys, but it was clear that they were allowing the smith to do the speaking. The sea captain — for the big man was certainly the ship's captain — watched them come, and then he smiled. He was standing on his afterdeck, which put him a man's height above the pier, able to look down on them from the rail.

"Morning to you, Master Smith," he rumbled. "Are you in need of more iron billets?"

The mooring ropes creaked. A little breeze had blown up from the land, and the fog was starting to shred away.

Loys squinted up at the ship in the strengthening sunlight. "Morning to you, Captain. Have any of your men been away from the ship this morning?"

The captain's eyebrows rose. He shook his head. "No. I have but four crew. All of them are here, as you see. They've been onboard since it was light enough to splice and mend sail." He glanced upwards at the clearing sky.

"We sail in a day or so, and a fool I'd be to let them idle in a tavern when there's storm damage to repair."

"No one has been up to the village, not even for a few minutes — when the fog was at its worst?"

The captain shrugged. "No. I keep my crew at work, when they work." The seamen grinned, but none disagreed. "What's this about?"

Loys stared him in the eyes. "Someone attacked my daughter just now, in the fog. She never saw him, but it could have been a try at a slave-taking." He leaned on his hammer, its heavy head by his foot. "It wouldn't have been the first time a Western Islander has taken slaves."

The captain folded his arms. "I am no slaver, Master Smith. I have no place to put slaves, as you see. No slave deck, no cage. And it is against your Queen's Law. I would lose my permit to trade to her lands if I carried them."

Loys nodded. "And your men? You vouch for them?"

"I do. Seek your child-taker elsewhere, Master Smith. It was no doing of ours."

"Rhianna?" asked Loys. He did not take his eyes from the sea-trader's face.

Rhianna looked hard at the redbearded captain, and slowly shook her head. "I don't know, Father. I . . . can't say."

"Very well. Thank you for your courtesy, Master Merchant. There is no more to say."

Loys took Rhianna's hand, and then turned and walked steadily away up the pier, towards the village street. The villagers parted to let them pass, and then followed them.

The captain stared thoughtfully after them, stroking a forefinger over his bearded chin. After a moment, he inclined his head to one of the seamen.

"Stay with the ship. Don't leave it. They'll be watching us now." The seaman nodded. The captain went on stroking his chin. "Just as well you did lose her. It was the wrong girl."

The seaman's eyes shifted from side to side. "She said she came from the smithy. She was wearing the cape. She's the right age. But she's a witch, all right. Called monsters to her aid."

"So you say. Although I think you might have seen nothing more than the fumes of last night's ale. But she's not Eldra, as anyone could plainly see. Anyone who looks at her. And now we may have missed our chance. We'll stay two more days, though. Something may come up. After that, the tale about storm damage will be wearing thin."

"Why must we stay at all? There are fat merchant

ships in the western passage, and rich cargoes for the taking."

"And Queen's ships to take us. Anyway, there is more here than a cargo or two. Hrothwil has sent us himself, for high reasons of state. There's fame and gold here, if we can take them."

"Fame. Pah! Can you eat it? Can you spend it?"

"Then take the gold, fool, if you want it. I am Kaldi, son of Willen, of the —"

"— blood of Tostig Red-hand. Yes, so I hear. I hope your fame will not get us all killed."

Kaldi said nothing, but stood by the rail, watching the clearing sky, and stroked his chin.

CHAPTER 4

Once she was home, it was just as Rhianna had thought it would be. Just as she had feared.

First, her mother made her wash and change her clothes, and inspected her for hurts and sore places. There was bruising around her ribs, where the man's arm had squeezed, but nothing as bad as the scrapes and cuts she often got just in playing. Her parents looked at each other with relief that nothing worse had happened. Her father hugged her, briefly.

Then the lecture started. Both her parents at once. *Be careful. Watch what you're doing. We can't be there to watch you all the time — it's a dangerous world, Rhianna. And what's this about taking your pendant off? You know you shouldn't do that. Magister Northstar said . . .*

And so on and so on. It did no good to protest that it was just as well she wasn't wearing the pendant, and that she'd never have been able to get free if she hadn't used the Wild Magic. Her mother only said that it wasn't the point, and that Rhianna had promised not to take it off. What would Magister Northstar say?

Their voices were sharp with worry, and angry and sad and confused all at the same time. It was as bad a lecture as Rhianna had ever heard, but that wasn't the worst of it.

No. The worst of it was that she had to endure it while Eriseth was there, trying to look as if she couldn't hear anything, staring out the window, saying nothing. Mother and Father were humiliating her in front of Eriseth, it seemed.

When supper was put on the table, Eriseth sat on the bench and fidgeted, and Rhianna had to sit next to her. There wasn't even Magister Northstar to talk to. Rhianna sat in silence, angry and glum, both at once.

At first, nobody said anything at all. Then Loys shook himself, remembering that he had a guest. He poured milk for Eriseth and ale for himself, and spoke lightly to Meg. "Mrs. Farmer stopped in to order that new set of firedogs, love. Just as you said she would."

Meg passed him more sausages and smiled in her turn, sensing his need to talk about something different. "You should see their fireplace, Loys, that they want the firedogs for. Berengia Farmer has been talking about it all winter, and it's just been finished. When I called by a few days ago to pick up some spinning wool, she showed it to me, proud as a queen. It's big enough to roast an ox in, with seats either side actually by the fire itself, and a chimney wide enough to climb up so it can be swept, and a fancy chimney pot on top to keep the rain out."

"Use a lot of firewood, something that size," said her husband, with his mouth full. He took a pull at his mug of ale.

"I don't think that would worry the Farmers. That's a fine big place they've got out there, and there's three strong sons to help work it . . ."

She broke off. There was no son in the Wildwood house to carry on the smithy, and Meg felt it badly. She knew how Loys wanted a son to hand his trade to. Counting her blessings, she looked across at Rhianna, but Rhianna was scowling down at the table as if she had a pain.

Loys simply reached across and touched his wife's hand for a moment. "That explains the size of the dogs they want for it. Three handspans high, and long enough to hold a full beech log." He held his hands apart, the width of his wide shoulders, to show the size. "Eriseth helped me hammer out the barstock for them today, and we can do the welding and the fine work tomorrow." He looked at his apprentice. "I'll show you some chisel work then, Eris. I've a feeling you'll do well with that."

Rhianna's lips twisted. She stared at her plate, and for the rest of the meal she said nothing.

The next day was Saturday — no school for Rhianna, though Loys Wildwood worked a half day in the forge. If the truth were known, he worked more than a half day, and Meg Wildwood tutted as the sun reached its peak and started to descend, and her husband had not returned.

"You'll have to take his dinner down to him, Rhianna," she said as she cleared the table. "He'll have gotten involved in something, but he'll need to eat." She packed a basket with cold beef and pickles and bread and butter.

"Oh, Mother, really! It's not my fault he hasn't come home. And it's cold and wet out. Why should I have to?"

Her mother bit her lip. "Rhianna, I know why you don't want to go out, but you have to, sometime. It's not foggy today. I'll watch you until the turn in the path, and from there it's only a few steps to the forge."

Rhianna pulled a face. Mother seemed to think that it was because of the business the day before that she didn't want to go out. But that wasn't the reason. The reason was Eriseth.

"I don't want to," she muttered.

"I know, but still, you must. Those Westerners haven't left their ship since yesterday, except the captain, and he only went as far as the little wood — hunting rabbits, he said. Everyone's watching them. It's broad daylight, Rhianna, no fog, and there's people about. Go on. Your father will be expecting you, and I have work to do."

So it was that Rhianna trudged slowly and resentfully down the path to the village street, turned left, and walked past the market on the green and down towards the little harbor. When she made the turn, she could see the ship tied up at the pier, where the street ended at the harbor wall. She passed the baker and the two ship's-chandler's shops, the ropemaker and the carpenter. And there was the smithy.

The smithy was a sort of a shed, really. A workbench ran around three walls, with tools — hammers and pincers, grips and files, gauges, cold-chisels — racked above it. Rhianna liked its sharp smells of hot coals and hot iron, and the warmth of the firelight. Especially at this time of year, when it seemed welcoming and comforting after the cold and damp outside. She paused for a moment in the street, though, reluctant. Then, telling herself that was silly, she went inside. It took her eyes a few seconds to get used to the dim light.

In the middle of the floor was Father's anvil — two of them, actually, one for fine work — and the forge itself, a long fire in a shallow brick tub, fed with pure charcoal and blown by a large pair of bellows. It was Saturday afternoon, and the fire should be drawn by now, but instead the bellows were still being worked — by Eriseth. In the fire was a long iron bar, and she was bringing it up hot. Her face was set with concentration. She hardly nodded as Rhianna came in. Of Loys Wildwood there was no sign at all.

"Where's your Master?" asked Rhianna. She didn't want to say "Father" to Eriseth.

"At the harbor. He wanted to see about some more billets." Eriseth didn't take her eyes off her work.

Rhianna sniffed. "Oh. Well, you can give him this when he comes back." She put down the basket, turned to go, and then stopped.

She hadn't noticed before — the smithy was dim, lit only by its fire — but as she swung around she saw them: a pair of firedogs, larger than she had ever seen before. Long, thin dogs made of bar-iron, meant to hold a big log in a fireplace. They had tails and noses that pointed up, and four lean legs to stand on. These were fancier firedogs than usual, their heads and paws sculpted out of the hot, glowing iron with cold-chisel work. Their long bodies were worked with patterns of hammer strokes to make their fur, and their mouths were open wide, as if panting in the heat, showing lolling tongues and sharp teeth. They had been chilled and tempered in the water-barrel, and now stood by the door, waiting for the blacking and annealing work that would keep them from rust.

Eriseth had apparently forgotten that Rhianna was there. Her hand in a padded glove, she drew the bar-iron from the fire. The end had already been hammered into a wedge shape. She clamped it, glowing orange, into a vice on the bench top, then shed the glove and took up a small hammer and a fine chisel. Striking once, twice, the chisel held at exact angles, she began to work a wolf's head into the hot end of the iron. Despite herself, Rhianna watched, fascinated.

Ears, then the open mouth, a few deft hammer strokes to narrow the muzzle to a point, which was then squared off with one cut. Then the punch, to make eyes and nostrils. The head emerged from the glowing metal under hands that were sure and skilled.

Rhianna felt she had to say something. "Did my fa — your Master . . . tell you to use his bar-iron for that?" she asked, and then sharply: "Only it costs money, you know. It's not for ornament."

Eriseth held up the work, its orange glow fading as it cooled and hardened. She plunged it, spluttering, into the water barrel. "He told me to practice the chisel work he showed me. I am doing as he said," she replied calmly. Her eyes glanced sideways at Rhianna, a flash of white in the red glow. "I am obeying, mistress, just as I obeyed my Wisewoman." She faced Rhianna. "Though it is not you that I swore to obey." She pulled the iron from the water barrel and inspected the head carefully. "The eyes are a little uneven," she muttered to herself.

"Not as good as my father's, then," said Rhianna. Her voice was cutting.

"No," said Eriseth. "Do you expect my work to be as good as his? You must have little respect for your father's skills." Rhianna opened her mouth to retort, but the Eldra girl nodded at the firedogs by the door. "Yet he had me do the hammer work on one of those, after showing me how, and he allowed it to stand, saying that it was as good as he could have done himself. It's not the most skilled part of the job, but . . ."

"No, it isn't. And he was just being polite," returned Rhianna hotly. To be told she had no respect! Who did this Eldra chit think she was?

Eriseth's brows lifted, and she inspected Rhianna coolly. "Indeed, and your father, my Master, is a *polite* man. None more so. A pity all his household cannot follow his lead. Yet, if he was only being polite, perhaps you would care to tell me which is the dog that I hammered and which is his."

Rhianna was furious now, hardly able to think what to say. "Why should I bother with that?"

Eriseth folded her arms. There were black sooty marks and a scorch or two on them, Rhianna saw, but the Eldra girl showed no discomfort. "Well, don't bother, then. No doubt you have far more important things to do than stand here talking to me. Why don't you just go away?"

Rhianna felt the fury bubble up inside her. "*Me* go away? I *live* here, not under some tree somewhere, like you! Why don't *you* go away, woods-runner?"

Eriseth's lips tightened. She said nothing, but Rhianna wasn't finished. She went on: "But, yes, I have got more important things to do, actually. If you want to know. I was just going to practice working some magic. Changing, summoning, restoring. You know, all those things *you* can't do at all." A flicker of pain passed across Eriseth's face, and Rhianna rejoiced. "Much more important things than standing here talking to you."

Eriseth closed her eyes and bowed her head. Then she thrust the bar into the forge again and began to pump the bellows. She did it harder than she needed to. "Go and be about it, then. I have work to do." She lifted her head and looked Rhianna in the eyes as she pulled on the glove. "It was what I was hired for. No soft words and hugs and sympathy for me. I have no magic, and want none, not when I have the iron. And unlike you, I obey my Master. So run along and play with your little magical *toys*, mistress. Some of us have more worthwhile things to learn." Her voice was as cool as the winter wind. She pulled the bar from the fire and turned away.

Rhianna recoiled as if she'd been slapped. "Toys?" she cried. "Toys, is it? I'll show you what I can do with *your* toys!"

She whipped the jewel on its chain over her head and dropped it. Power surged in from the fire and the wind, the ground and the sea itself. The Wild Magic filled her like a wave, roaring in her ears, in her blood. She looked about swiftly, and then pointed at the long iron bar in Eriseth's hand.

"I'll make a really *good* toy for you, elf! Watch this!" Enraged, Rhianna took the Wild Magic and formed it and shaped it, and she sent her anger and her will to the iron to tell it what it should be. She wanted a strong sending, and in her fury she wasn't in the mood to be careful.

Eriseth's eyes switched from the iron to Rhianna's face. "No!" she shouted, but it was lost in Rhianna's boiling rage. And then a dreadful thing happened.

The wolf's head that was worked in the glowing metal shook itself, and its mouth opened. Its tongue lolled out, panting in the heat of its own forging, and then the little slit eyes glowed like hotter points. Its lips rose, it showed red-hot teeth, it snarled like a saw striking a nail, and it snapped at Eriseth.

She cried out, and the rod seemed to writhe in her grip. She might have dropped it, and nobody knows what would have happened if she had. Would it have been a living iron wand with a wolf's head, and would it have bitten her with its red-hot teeth?

But Eriseth held on to the metal, and she turned and thrust the bar into the water barrel to quench it. There was a howl and a huge bubbling and hissing. Eriseth let go of the bar and jumped back as it lashed itself backwards and forwards in the barrel like a snake.

She turned furiously on Rhianna. "You little fool, what have you —? Oh, no!"

"Just showing you what *real* magic is like, apprentice, because you don't know anything about it. Just giving you something to think about. And I can do it anytime . . ."

But Eriseth wasn't looking at her. She was staring at the open door, and there was horror on her face. Rhianna heard a crackling and a creaking, as of iron hinges grating open. She turned, and her mouth popped open. Her eyes opened wide with shock.

For the firedogs were twitching, bending, then turning on their long lean legs to look at her. The hammered fur on their necks rose in iron spikes like a ruff, and they growled, both of them together, a noise like a file being drawn over an iron bar. Sharp iron teeth showed in their iron jaws, and their little eyes were red-hot points like glowing metal. They lifted their iron paws with a clink and a jerk, and sidled towards the door.

Even in her shock, Rhianna knew that she had to repair this thing, and that it had to be done straight away. She gathered her magic to uncast the spell, and as she did so, the dogs seemed to realize what she was going to do.

In an instant they had dashed through the open front of the smithy and out into the street. Rhianna, horrified, lurched into a run after them, Eriseth close behind her. Too late!

The dogs were in the street in a flash. One turned right, towards the market. The other went the other way, downhill, towards the sea. Rhianna gasped, dithered, and then sprinted after the one going uphill. Nearly everyone was at the market. The dog would have the most chance of doing harm there. She put her head down and ran.

But the dog was faster. It ran between legs and baskets. It slid under tables and around counters. Rhianna blundered on, trying to keep it in sight, yet knowing that she was falling further behind. Eriseth was no better. She was used to the forest, not to crowded marketplaces. By the time they emerged on the other side, the dog was only a black loping dot on the hillface in front of them.

Rhianna ran until she could run no farther. At last she drew to a stop, blowing and heaving, on the sharp slope above the village. Before her were the dark woods, and somewhere in that expanse of trees the iron dog had disappeared. She could only stare after it. Slowly it grew on her that she had done a dreadful thing. Eriseth came up behind her, bow in hand, arrow on string.

"Well," said Eriseth, "that's trouble. I'm not following it without food and gear."

"The other one, then," said Rhianna, and they trotted all the way back, grimly silent. Through the marketplace and down the street once more. Past the smithy, still empty and silent, with Loys Wildwood nowhere in sight, and on towards the harbor.

There was the Western Islander ship, still tied up at the pier. A sailor came to the rail with a pail of slops and stopped, watching them.

"Hola, missy," he called. "Been captured by slavers again, have you?"

Rhianna ignored the question. "Did you see a dog?" she asked. "A long, thin dog. It might have come past here."

The sailor scratched his beard. "Dog?" he asked, as if she had inquired about a sea serpent. "No dog. Does he swim, like? Only I saw what I thought was a seal, oh, a little while back. Must have been a seal. A pup, maybe. Jumped in the water off the harbor wall just there. I only saw it jump. Didn't see it come up. They can go a long way underwater, seals." Another sailor's head appeared over the rail. "I said to Gunnar, here, that's a funny place to see a seal, I said, and he said . . ."

"I said it weren't no seal. No seal hereabouts, I said."

"Well, it must have been a seal, Gunnar Ragnusson, say I, 'cause for why? 'Cause it weren't no dog, say I, no, nor cat neither, jumping off the wall into the sea like that . . ."

Rhianna turned away and left them to it. She trailed slowly up the deserted street, with Eriseth behind her.

When they arrived at the smithy, there was still no Loys Wildwood.

They looked at each other.

"He might have gone home, looking for us," said Rhianna, and they both climbed the slope towards Rhianna's house.

And indeed he was there, in a chair, his legs propped on a stool. Meg was examining a long scratch on his calf, just below the knee. No. It wasn't a scratch. It was a cut, a nasty one, fresh, still bleeding.

He looked up as they came in. "'Lo, Rhianna, Eriseth. What do you think? A dog runs between my legs, just as I'm coming back from bargaining with that Westerner in the harbor. I don't think he's serious about selling, by the way — the price he wanted for iron billets! A waste of time, and then this. Ow!" Meg was trying to staunch the bleeding with a linen bandage, but the wound kept dripping steadily. "The dog must have been wearing a spiked collar. Or he's got really sharp teeth. It all happened in a moment, but he got me a good one. I'd tell his owner a thing or two, but I don't know who it is. I've seen the dog before, though, somewhere." He looked at Eriseth. "And where have those firedogs gotten to? I looked for you, Eris, as I passed by the smithy, but you'd gone, and so had they."

CHAPTER 5

Rhianna stood and watched Magister Northstar's face. She tried to watch her father's, and her mother's, as well. She could not see Eriseth, who stood behind her, but she knew that her face, too, was lined with sorrow, and that her tears also fell. Rhianna wished that she could simply stare at the kitchen floor, the way she used to do, but she knew that now it would only make matters worse, if that were possible.

In fact, she wished that she were miles away, and that she could take back what had happened, but she knew that was something beyond her power. Even the Wild Magic couldn't call deeds back again and unmake the past. So she stood and watched them, and the fat, hot tears slid down her cheeks, and neither she nor the others took much notice of them. They all knew that this was one of those things that was so horrible and so enormous that it didn't much matter how sorry you were afterwards.

"How did you do it, Rhianna?" asked her Master. Her parents just looked at her, their eyes full of worry and sorrow. And there was pain, also, in her father's face. The cut was worse, hot and dark, and it kept weeping blood, not healing.

Rhianna shook her head, and the tears trickled faster. She smeared them with the back of her hand. Her mother passed her a handkerchief. They were still watching her, and she had to answer. "I was so *angry* at her. I had to do something. I had to show her that I could do things she couldn't." She heard her own voice, almost with disbelief, and Eriseth drawing a long, ragged breath behind her.

Magister Northstar pushed the words away with a gesture. "Child, child, we can all do things others can't. And others can do things we can't. That's part of not being all the same. But that's not what I asked you. I know you were angry, and I think I know why, and that it's my fault, or partly."

"And mine," put in Eriseth. "I had taken her rightful place, and I taunted her about it. I . . . I just envied her so much."

Rhianna looked at her in disbelief. "Envied me? *Me?* How? Why? What could you want . . ."

"You have so much. Magic, yes, but more . . . people

who love you, and will go on loving you no matter what you do. I have no magic, and my Home Grove, well, they said I shouldn't live there if I had none. Arwenna was good to me, and tried to find me a different craft, but still." She paused, and her face showed the strain. "We . . . the Eldra do not live as you do, in families, in settled houses. We move and we live for ourselves alone. Children are rare among us, for we live long lives. A man and a woman will stay together as long as a child needs both to feed it, but will go their own ways afterwards. Boys go with their fathers, girls with their mothers, and even then only as long as is needed to teach the child to live in the woods. And then, nothing. They might be hunting partners for a while, but more often they simply part. If they see each other again, it is as no more than people who are not complete strangers."

Rhianna looked at her, horrified. No mother? No father? How could anyone live in such a way? She turned appalled eyes on her Master.

Magister Northstar nodded. "Yes. So it is, among the Eldra. Their ways are not our ways. But I asked you a question, Rhianna, and it was not *why* you did this thing. I think I know why. I want to know *how*."

Rhianna shook her head, not understanding. The Magister slumped into a chair. He seemed tired. It took a day and a half, normally, to cross to Home Island by ship, but he had raised the Wizard's Wind in the sails to come as fast as may be, called by the spellcaster he'd given Rhianna long before. He had done it in barely ten hours, arriving in the early evening, and the effort of bending even the winds to his will had told on him. He wasn't a young man anymore.

"*How* is important, Rhianna," he said. "Somehow or other, you bespelled cold iron. Now, that . . . is supposed to be impossible. Cold iron is supposed to be immune to magic." He took off his tall wizard's hat and put it on the kitchen table in front of him. "It might be the anger. Anger is a fire-caller, and iron is made in the fire. But I don't know how it was done. I didn't think it *could* be done. All of Wizardly College thought it couldn't be done. Worse, the Queen's Council thought it couldn't be done — because we wizards told them so." He looked up. "But here I am, and it has been done. And now I have to tell the Council that we were wrong all along, and that I've given them bad advice."

Rhianna wiped her face again. "I . . . I don't understand," she faltered at last.

The Magister grunted. It might have been a laugh, the sort of laugh that says *This isn't very funny, but if I don't laugh, I'll do something worse.* "Loys? Have you ever had an order for a magic sword?"

Rhianna's father shook his head. He looked pale and

ill. "I'm no swordsmith, Magister. I know how to work the metal, but . . . a magic sword, you say?"

"Just suppose, then. Suppose you could make a blade, a fine blade, and then have it bespelled — so that it never lost its edge, was light as a willow wand, and carved through shield and armor like paper. How much do you think a pirate, or a warlord, or an enemy king would pay for such a thing?"

Loys said nothing, but his face went still. He glanced at Meg. But the Magister hadn't finished. His voice grew quiet, and yet it held them, as if it had hands. This was the Wizard's Voice, the voice that stills others, the voice that must be heard. "Worse. Worse. What would such a person do to take control of the way of making such things? Hmm? What would he *not* do? To become the only ruler in the world able to wield a magic sword? What would be the first thing he would think of doing, if he knew that there was one person in the world able to make such a sword? Do you not think that he would seek her out? Aye, and do whatever he had to, to *make* her give it to him?"

He looked from face to face in the appalled silence that followed, and nodded grimly. "There are such folk about. King Hrothwil, over on Westoway, for one. Wouldn't he just love to have a way to beat the Queen's army and plunder Home Island? Some of the Windlords of Glasheel are as bad. And even among the Eldra there are those who, shall we say, would welcome bespelled steel." He stared through the open window into the darkness, as if insuring that the people he named were not in sight. "You see. So they must not hear of it. Perhaps we can still hold the secret in this room." He looked around at Eriseth and Rhianna. "You have not told anyone else what happened? And no one else saw?"

"No, Magister," said Rhianna. "The sailors said they saw nothing. The dog might have jumped into the sea, though. But the ship's sailed now. And there was no one else around, down by the harbor."

"But many people in the market saw the other dog, Magister," said Eriseth. "They will talk."

"So they will. But so long as they don't understand that the dog was really made of iron, it won't matter much. A dog loose at a village market makes no great story, even if it runs very fast and seems hard to catch. Loys, I am sorry for the loss of your work. Can you make another pair of firedogs? I will pay you for your labor."

"Of course, Magister, when I'm on my feet again, and there'll be no pay involved."

"Yes, there is. I am responsible to other Masters for the deeds of my apprentice."

"Not only *your* apprentice. They were both in it, as Eris says, and I am not without fault here, myself . . . but we can work this out later. What's to be done with them now?"

Silence. Rhianna's tears came again. "I suppose," she faltered, "you should make me stay in my room for a month . . ."

"What good would that do?" asked Magister Northstar. "You need to be working on your control of your magic, not be shut up in your room. No, no. That's not enough, not enough at all. I have a far worse punishment in mind for you, Rhianna."

Rhianna wet her lips. What could be a worse punishment? Her parents had never taken a birch rod to her, not even at the worst. She could only watch the Magister and listen to what he said, because he was still her Master, and her apprenticeship oath to him held her as surely as the Wizard's Voice. More surely, in fact, because the Voice was only his magic, and might be broken by a stronger power, but her oath was partly her own magic, and not to be broken by itself.

"No," the Magister continued. "A far heavier punishment than that." He leaned forward. "I require that you grow up, young lady, and that you do it fast. You always had to, you know. You have power beyond your years; so you must *act* beyond your years, too. And part of that is to know the evil you have done, and to repair it yourself. Not ask me, or your parents, or anyone else to do it for you. To do it yourself. That is what is meant by 'taking re-sponsibility.' Grown-up people take responsibility for what they do."

Rhianna swallowed. The tears hadn't mattered be-fore; now they mattered less. She made to speak, thought, then tried again. Finally, she said, "I don't know how, Magister."

"No. Nor did you know how you made the magic in the first place. But you must find out. And you, too, Eriseth. If this is partly your doing, then its mending is partly on you, too. You must work together."

Rhianna looked back to see Eriseth's face. The Eldra eyes, slanted, dark, stared back at her. Without shifting her gaze, she nodded. "Yes, Magister."

Eriseth nodded, too. "Yes, Magister."

Magister Northstar rubbed his eyes. "And now let me see that leg of yours, Loys."

"Gunnar is dead," said the seaman. "Died just now. Fevered, raving."

Kaldi leaned against the tiller. The coast was just in sight to port, and the *Raven* had a brisk nor'-east breeze on her quarter. Smallhaven lay a day behind her. He con-sidered, and then spoke.

"He lost a finger to the thing. Clean bitten off. It wouldn't stop bleeding."

The other spat over the leeward rail. "Aye. He was a hard man, though. A man doesn't die of losing a finger. I say we throw the thing overboard. Let it bite on the fishes."

"And I say it stays. We took enough trouble over it. We'd never have done it at all if we hadn't had the spare cargo net and the chain cable. But it'll be worth it. Hrothwil will fill our hands with gold for this, and twice over for the other one, and more still if we can bring him the chit who bespelled the iron. Would you heave all that into the sea?"

"I would rather have less gold and be alive to spend it."

"It's safe enough for now."

"Aye, for now. But it keeps biting through its bonds. Only chains hold it. What if it takes it into its head to bite through the ship's keel instead? We could all find ourselves in the Sea-hag's Palace at the bottom of the ocean."

Kaldi grinned. "You nearly ended up there last month, in the storm. You chose the roving life, and it's often a short one. If a little risk upsets you, go back to your father's farm and tend his cattle. For me, Kaldi, son of Willen, it will be renown, not safety."

"Storms and arrows and war are all fair enough. An iron hound is uncanny. You'll see. It'll bring a curse on us."

"If it be the curse of having too much gold or fame, I

am willing to chance it." Kaldi looked up at the sail. "The Eldra scout said the creek mouth where we'll meet her mistress is about here. We'll go in to the coast. As soon as we're on the new course, we'll put Gunnar over the side."

CHAPTER 6

"Father's worse, isn't he?" Rhianna hated to ask, but she had to know.

Magister Northstar's robe was crumpled. It was the following morning, but he hadn't been to bed. Rhianna had heard his voice in the night, chanting the healing spells. He pursed his lips, so that he looked as though he were sucking on a lemon. "Wounds like that often sicken before they heal," he said.

"And sometimes they don't heal at all," said Rhianna.

The wizard made no reply. He leaned his staff on the table and sat wearily.

They were three in the warm kitchen, with its bright pans and solid table. Eriseth stood by the door, her bow-stave in her band. Meg Wildwood was in the bedroom, trying to get Loys to eat some soup.

Rhianna spoke again. "It's the dog. It must be the dog. The wound's poisoned, isn't it?"

The Magister sighed. "Poisoned. Yes, I'm afraid it is. My spells take no hold. Feverstay and healing make no difference. It feels as though I am spending strength, and yet it drains away into a great void that is larger than my strength and his combined. I don't know if the void can be closed."

"It's my fault." Rhianna whispered it, and she knew it was true. But the wizard shook his head.

"It's the fault of us all. I was a fool, and I ignored you while I chased old memories. Eriseth bitterly envied you. You were jealous, and your father tried to make of Eriseth the son he never had, while neglecting the daughter he did have. We all made the dogs, and they left something of themselves in the wound. What was it that went into them? Fire and iron, envy and jealousy, and rage and bitter gall. Fear and foolishness, ignorance and neglect. Is there any wonder the wound is poisoned, with such things in it? And there's the Wild Magic, too, and there I have no power at all."

There was a silence. The last words hung in the air. *The Wild Magic.* Rhianna's chin rose. "Is there any cure?" she asked, and mingled with the pain and sorrow was something else. The Wild Magic was *her* magic. She had never asked for it, but she owned it, and she was its mistress. If Magister Northstar had no power, then it was for her to have the power.

He looked up and stared into her eyes. "I don't know.

I know this — that in every poison is its own cure. Find the poison and unmake it, and there is the cure. More than that, I cannot say."

Rhianna stood, and her face was different, somehow. The pain was still there, and would always be there, but now there was something else to go with it: a great calm, or perhaps an unburdening. Now she knew what she must do. "Find the poison. Yes, Magister. I had better be about the hunt, then. And I know one who is a better hunter than I." She turned to Eriseth. "We go hunting, Eriseth Arwensgrove. One of the dogs, at least, has left a trail that we can follow. We hunt together."

Eriseth nodded. "Aye, Rhianna Wildwood. We hunt together. And I am glad to hunt with you."

Beyond the village fields, the hills struck up. The trees of the forest came down in swathes and long fingers in the heavier soil of the valleys between, and men had started the work of clearing there and making fields for crops. There were farms now in the nearer valleys, but beyond that the trees ruled, as they had for time out of mind.

Rhianna and Eriseth stood where the dog had gone into the forest, and Eriseth pored over the ground under the trees where it had disappeared. She bent suddenly, then straightened. "Here," she said, and pointed. "The tracks lead away up the hill."

Her gesture led the eye away into the fastness of the trees. Rhianna looked at the ground doubtfully. Here under the canopy of the forest she could see only a few smudges in the leaf mold that covered the ground, and they could have been anything or nothing. She had to take Eriseth's word that these were tracks at all, and she had seen nothing on the hard, thin soil of the hill.

"Have you not eyes?" asked Eriseth, wonder in her voice. "Look there . . . and there." She pointed, and Rhianna saw nothing but what might have been vague shadows on the ground. "Not only that, either. The grasses are bent . . . here, and here. There's a crushed stem there . . . leaves that have been thrust aside. That oak has been scraped past — see the mark? The dog has blundered along like a wheel of stone, leaving traces a blind man could follow. We can track it to its lair."

Rhianna looked harder where she was pointing. "The tracks lead straight into the woods, then?"

The Eldra girl nodded.

"How far?"

Eriseth smiled and shook her head. "Now you ask me to say the impossible. I cannot tell where the lair might be."

"How do you know it will have a lair at all?"

"All wild things have a lair."

Rhianna frowned. She was not to know such things,

and there was a certainty in Eriseth's voice that reassured. And yet . . . these were not wild animals, not really. They had been made from iron and anger and magic, and there was no way to say what they really were. She did not know herself what they were, and if she who had made them didn't know, who could?

Rhianna had asked Magister Northstar if he would come with them, but the wizard had shaken his head, unsmiling. "This is your doing, and yours must be the undoing, both of you. What use would I be? I am not to tell Eriseth of the ways of the woods, for she knows them far better than any of us. Nor am I to tell you, Rhianna, of the Wild Magic. Anyway, I am old and have trouble enough where the paths are clear. I would only slow you down. Besides, I have a charge and a patient here." There was a cry of pain from the other room. He turned to go back in, to begin the healing song again. "Go on your way, then, and luck go with you."

So Rhianna had followed Eriseth, as Eriseth now followed the trail that Rhianna could not see. Up the hill they went, then down the other side, and into the forest. Here, where the leaf litter was deep under the trees, the marks were plain enough, even to Rhianna. She followed the trail, and the Eldra girl moved ahead of her like a shadow, the strung bow in her hand. They began the hunt, looking forward into the shadows of the great trees, and it never occurred to either of them to watch behind.

Beyond the range of hills there was a valley that Rhianna had not expected, a wide, shallow one that ran parallel with the lines of rising ground. Beyond that again the hills rose into mountains, now invisible in the mist. The weather had closed in again, and it came on to rain, a soft, chilling drizzle. Rhianna was glad of her oiled-wool cape and hood and her soft boots that her mother had worked with dubbin against the damp.

It rained on and off, chill and penetrating, and mist curled its cold fingers around the trees. The weather grew bleaker and more gray. Colors were dim and muted, as if the forest were seen through smoked glass.

Silent to Rhianna's ears, Eriseth moved among the trees, and Rhianna thought that it was as if they walked in a dream, one of those where everything is indefinite and hard to see. In such dreams there is always a thing that has to be done, something urgent and important, though sometimes you forget what that thing is. She set herself to follow the Eldra girl, treading in her footprints, watching how she walked, staying back as she studied the ground, going on as she found the trail again. They moved on, deeper into the winter-silent woods, and Rhianna found her thoughts shifting like the sap rising in the trees.

Standing close as soldiers in ranks, the trees had always appeared to her before like a hostile army, dark, forbidding, closed. Now they seemed at worst neutral, as if they were watching her out of ancient, wise eyes, making a slow assessment of her and of her magic. She knew, suddenly, that to them she must be like an insect, a fragile, short-lived thing that flitted past and was gone without trace in a moment.

On and on they went, until at last Eriseth cocked her head as if hearing a faint sound, and then nodded to herself. She moved on, down a gentle slope, among trees that were different — alders and rowans, not oaks. After a while Rhianna could hear the sound for herself. It was the roll and ripple of water, flowing somewhere at the bottom of the slope.

Through thickets and brush they pushed their way, water flicking from the twigs, until they came to the banks of the river. Eriseth beckoned Rhianna up to stand beside her. The brush grew right down to the water's edge, but in places there were stones set so close that not even a thousand summers of root and growth had been able to dislodge them. A boulder the size of a house jutted out into the river, which swirled and bubbled around it, urgent in late winter spate. Eriseth stood on it, leaning on her bowstave. She nodded across the swift stream.

"It crossed here," she said. "The tracks are fresh. And the lair is close. It has already come far, and it would be near water. Iron though it may be, it is a dog, too." Her voice was low, a murmur that carried to Rhianna's ears only.

Rhianna held up a wetted finger. The cold little wind was in their faces. Eriseth nodded at the gesture.

"Yes," she said. "Well thought. The wind blows from it to us. Good. But I think it knows we are on the track, anyway. Though what it can scent, or how, I have no idea."

Rhianna gazed over the hurrying water. "Can we cross here?"

"Yes. There's a ford, good even now. The question is, should we?" Cold rain pattered down between her words. It beaded on the hood of Rhianna's cape, and she shook the drops off.

"Do we have a choice?" she asked.

Eriseth picked up her bow. "No," she replied, briefly. "I'll go first. There's a pothole halfway over. Step where I step."

She bundled her shoes and stockings together and rolled them in her cloak. That went on her head, with the bowstave struck through the bundle like a giant hairpin.

Rhianna imitated her, and then followed in her footsteps as she let herself down into the stream. She wondered how Eriseth knew this crossing so well, but, as with wizards, she felt it best not to ask questions about Eldra knowledge.

Eriseth nodded, as if she understood what Rhianna was thinking. Almost she smiled. "The river marks the boundary of the Eldra lands," she said. "We know it well. We should. Your Queen's Council made the treaty, and we have kept it. In fairness, so have you." She climbed the shelving bank. "Welcome to the lands of my people," she said.

Rhianna stopped, ten paces behind her. For an instant she hesitated, uncertain both of her footing, and because she was leaving the lands of the Queen. But a nod from Eriseth told her where the hole lurked in the bed of the stream, and she moved again, circling it carefully, her feet already numb with the cold. The current tugged at her, but the water never crept higher than her thighs. By leaning into it, she could keep her feet.

With relief she felt the ground start to shelve. The stream lapped at her knees and calves, and at last she crunched over pebbles. There was a steep bit of bank, but Eriseth climbed it and then offered the end of her bow-stave to help her out. Rhianna took it gladly. She was starting to shiver. Once at the top, she began to pull on her clothing again, grateful that it was still fairly dry.

Cold leaches strength from a person, making her slow of wit and dull of hearing. Rhianna heard nothing. Eriseth gasped and whirled, and her fingers plucked an arrow from the quiver at her belt. In a second she had drawn it to her ear, for there was something reddish-brown among the red-brown leaves on the ground, something that moved at a stiff lope. Eriseth held the arrow and stared at it.

Rhianna could not move or think. The dog stopped and lifted its head stiffly, as if to test the air, and it stared at them. The iron spikes of its fur rose on its neck, and its little eyes still held the red heat of the fire in which it had been forged. They stared into Rhianna's eyes like hot coals. She swallowed, and tried to fight down her fear. Of itself her hand went to the jewel about her neck, and of itself lifted it over her head, and dropped it to the ground.

She drew the cold of winter about her like her cloak — snow and ice, rain and mist to counter the fire. Water-magic, flowing, swift, mobile, to set against the hardness and endurance of the iron. The Wild Magic leaped up, ready to burst forth in a torrent, and with it came the urge to hurl it wholesale against the iron dog as it crouched in the leaves of last autumn, among the dark boles of the trees.

But she struggled against the urge and against her fear. If she let her Wild Magic do as it would, what might she let loose on the world this time? Ice tigers, perhaps? She might even bring the Frost Giants back again, the Cold Ones who once rode the rivers of ice as if they were war horses, at the very dawn of the world. She must keep the Wild Magic within bounds. And as she thought that, it was as if the magic was reined in, like a horse obeying the hands and knees of a good rider. Her head stayed clear. She watched the dog instead, trying to see what made it what it was, trying to see how it might be unmade.

It opened iron jaws and snarled in its voice of steel rasping on steel. Rhianna could see its teeth, and she knew, with a spurt of renewed fear, that weapons would not stop it, and that behind herself and Eriseth there was nothing but the roaring river.

The dog grinned its terrible grin and started to move towards them, still snarling, eyes red-hot, moving slowly and stiffly.

Slowly and stiffly.

Rhianna blinked. Her mouth opened. Suddenly, she saw the dog for the first time. She had seen it, but had not truly *seen* before. Eriseth was looking back at her, uncertain, retreating from it as it moved stiffly in the wet mold, but Rhianna kept her eyes on the dog. All at once she knew why it was the color of the dead leaves.

Rhianna Wildwood was her father's daughter, brought up within the sight and sound of the forge. Her oldest memories were of the ring of hammer on anvil and the glow of charcoal. She knew iron, she knew what made it, and she knew what could unmake it. It was nothing to be frightened of, even though she had abused it and must now repair what she had done. She called on the Wild Magic, but little — little — binding it to her will, making it do as she required, and not as it would.

Eriseth saw the dog blink and shake its head, puzzled. Its movement slowed. It halted in its advance and pushed out its head as though trying to loosen its shoulders for the spring forward. It did the same for each limb in turn, stretching them as if the joints were painful, bending from side to side. Then its head came up. It stared at Rhianna, and it was as if sudden understanding came into its hot eyes. Stiffly it turned, and there was the sound of rough metal grinding against itself. It burrowed into the bushes, and a sparkle of drops came cascading down as it crashed through. More crackles and the scrape of iron against twigs told where it went on.

Rhianna let out a long breath that she hadn't known she was holding in. She stooped, scooped up the jewel from the ground and slipped it into a pocket, where it did not touch her skin. The magic around her blinked and flickered like the sun off a crow's wing, stuttered and returned.

"Quick!" she called. "Follow it!"

CHAPTER 7

The dog could still be heard scraping and burrowing in the bushes, over the sound of the rain. Pushing wet branches out of the way, Rhianna and Eriseth followed it. Thorns and sharp twigs caught on their clothes, slowing them, and drops of water showered down on them as they went. After a while, only Eriseth could hear the crackle and rustle somewhere up ahead, but still they went on as quickly as they could. Rhianna felt the urgency, for she knew it must be finished soon, but Eriseth was cautious and careful as a hunter must be, watching for an ambush, knowing that she followed an animal that was hurt and dangerous.

It was caution that wasn't needed, at the end. They came to a blackberry patch, and as they sidled through the thorn-laden branches, Eriseth held up a hand. They stood still while she listened, head sidelong.

"It has come out into the clear again, perhaps fifty

paces ahead," she murmured. She listened again. "And now it has stopped moving."

Rhianna nodded. It was a dog, after all, and dogs are hunters of the plains. It had made for open ground, where it would feel less enclosed. In so far as it lived at all, it lived in the way a dog lives. Wild, for that was the magic. It was difficult to control and impossible to tame. But still it was a dog.

Again she gathered the Wild Magic around her like a cloak. It rose from the ground, and she could feel its power in the echo from the river, still close by. Above all, the magic stirred in the forest around her, beginning to wake from its winter sleep. Earth-magic from the ground, water-magic from the river. Fire-magic, faint and dry, from the cloud-covered sun. And life-magic, strongest of all, from the rising sap in the trees and the quickening of little minds all around her: the mice in their burrows, the winter birds, even the first insects that had begun to test the air as the cold loosened its grip.

Eriseth was watching her, questions in her face. Rhianna nodded. She was ready.

They went on.

The blackberry thicket ended with a piece of stony ground, a small height. There was a wide cap of rock, and on top of that a few boulders had been piled higgledy-piggledy by the frost: a good place for playing king-of-the-castle. Below it, oak trees stood dripping and silent in the wan light, packed close together like an audience to watch a play.

The hunters came into the open cautiously, watching the shadows. In the center of the clearing the iron dog stood and waited for them.

Here it had chosen to make its stand. The earth-magic was very strong here, where the rocks broke through the soil. That might have drawn the dog, for earth and fire had made it, with magic. Among the rocks on the stony ground was a place — not quite a burrow, more a sort of lean-to where two flat plates of stone were thrust against each other. Here, in the break between them, was its lair. Here it had brought dead leaves and piled them into a bed out of the wind, and done what it could to make a shelter. Here it faced them. It would retreat no further.

Now, slowly and stiffly, it came forward. Reluctant, snarling in its steel-file voice, yet it came. It knew Rhianna's power, and yet it would face her. Perhaps it, too, wanted it to be finished.

Rhianna watched it come, and she saw how it was and how it must become. She called water and fire to her aid; but even as she called she had to speak, for the life of the forest around her demanded that she explain herself and what she was doing. She had given this thing a semblance of the forest's own life, and now she must take it away again. It was a dreadful thing to have to do. She had to excuse what she did and what she had done, and hope for understanding.

"It's rusting, you see," she said softly, with pity. "That's why it's all reddish-brown. All iron rusts, if you leave it out in the damp. That would be the end of it, if we left it long enough. If we were cruel enough to let it slowly rot away. All I am doing is making it happen faster. As fast as I can, as fast as may be."

Eriseth nodded, watching. Her face was calm, reflective. She knew that a wounded animal, or one old or sick beyond hope, was owed this one favor. Her lips began to move silently, forming the words of the oldest of the chants of the Eldra, the chant that explains to the animal why it has been hunted, thanks it for its life, asks its pardon and blesses it on its way. And Rhianna called on the Wild Magic.

The dog ground to a halt twenty paces short of them, its stiff limbs no longer carrying it forward. Its head was being pulled back, and its hot eyes stared into Rhianna's own. She swallowed and stared back. This was required of her. It was her anger and her abuse of her talent that had loosed this on the world. She had done this thing. It was for her to look it in the eyes as she undid it.

The dog had become rigid, dull red-brown all over. It

was now of the same form as it had been when it came out of the forge, lean, standing four-square on its thin legs, its head and tail in the air. Now the pitting and corrosion of the rust ate into its body, spreading and deepening as they watched. Rhianna poured out the Wild Magic, using it fast so that it would be quickly over, her face closing in, her eyes narrowing.

The dog shivered once, or perhaps it was only a sigh. Then the hot light left its eyes, and they were suddenly blank, unseeing once more. It was iron again, simply old iron rusted into uselessness by having been left out in the rain. Still Rhianna called on the Wild Magic, to make sure, and the iron body lurched and then toppled over as a leg crumbled into flakes of rust. Moments later there was nothing but corroded pieces of iron, a red-black pile on the stone.

Eriseth moved forward. She reached the little pile of fragments and squatted on her heels, then stretched out her bowstave to stir them. There was a soft, wet sound, and the flaked rust fell in against itself.

Rhianna, for her part, didn't know whether to collapse from weariness or burst into tears. All magic has its price. The Wild Magic is no different. She felt as weary as she had ever felt, and in her weariness she had forgotten all other things around her.

She breathed out, long and ragged. Her shoulders slumped. "It's done,"' she said. "One, at least. Perhaps it will be enough to help Father."

But Eriseth was looking past her, over her shoulder and into the trees, and her face was rigid with shock.

"Aye," said a new voice. Rhianna whirled about. She had not seen the woman in the long gray-green woolen cloak before. Eldra, certainly: clear hazel eyes and clean of limb, long and lean and dark-haired. And the bow was Eldra, too, as long as she was, with the arrow on the string, held ready to bend and loose at a moment.

She stepped into the clearing, moving easily past the last trees. "And it was well done, too." The voice was light, mocking. "No, Eriseth Arwensgrove, leave your bow alone. Put it aside and stand where I can see your hands."

Eriseth did not move, still squatting by the crumbled remains of the iron dog. She had regained control of her face. "I do not think you will have time to shoot twice before one of us is on you, Gorsayd the Shadow. And you might miss. You were never the greatest of archers. Though it is true that in hiding and sneaking there are few to match you. I didn't see you or hear you at all, that much I do give you."

"Your ears and eyes have been dulled by your forge, Eriseth. I've been with you for more than a week. You're not much better than the Clumsy Ones. Indeed, you're one of them now. But you never were Eldra in your heart, nor was your Wisewoman, either. Now stand, and leave your bow where it is."

Eriseth shook her head. "I think not. Can you take both of us, when one of us has the Wild Magic?"

Rhianna watched and listened, astonishment growing. What was going on here?

"Who is this?" she asked Eriseth while watching the other.

Eriseth smiled, a showing of the teeth. "Rhianna Wildwood, meet Gorsayd Merchedsgrove, called the Shadow because she is dark and silent. She is one who dislikes your folk and wishes to be rid of them."

"As any true Eldra does," said Gorsayd, between clenched teeth.

"As any fool does who thinks that time and the world stand still. I will not do a fool's bidding. And now you must shoot, and you get only one shot." Eriseth's legs tightened under her, ready to hurl her to either side of the arrow's flight, if it should come.

Rhianna gathered her wits, and she gathered the Wild Magic around her. She would take her lead from Eriseth, and it was clear that Eriseth would defy this person. But the Magic would take care of that. *We'll see how this Gorsayd manages with a fog over her eyes . . .*

There was a new voice, quick and clear. "But I get a

shot, too. And I will match my magic against that of your Clumsy friend, Eriseth."

It was Eriseth's turn to snap her head around. Another newcomer, also armed with a bow, stepped out from among the trees. Another woman in a dark cloak, but a finer one, with silver at her throat and silver strands in her hair.

Eriseth's smile became bitter. "Merched the Wise herself. I might have known you would be here, where there is strife. Strife calls you as nectar calls the bee."

"If it be strife to wish our forests unfelled and our lives our own, then here am I, to strive for it. So I should. You and Arwenna would turn us into Clumsy Ones, like yourselves. And she would rule over us all, with the aid of your cold iron."

"Iron is but iron, Merched Strifeseeker. It is only a better stone."

Merched shook her dark head and thrust a hand out as if to push the words away. "No. It is an axe for our trees, a plow for our hunting grounds, and a knife at our throats. I want none of it. But here I have a way of ridding us of it."

Eriseth's eyebrows rose. "So? You would murder us here, then? That would mean war with Rhianna's folk. She is the apprentice of —"

"— Serenir the Wizard, of their Queen's Council.

Did you think we didn't know that? So, no, we will not kill you. In fact, your lives are very safe, indeed, for they are worth a great deal." She smiled in her turn, and then moved her head without taking her eyes off them. Raising her voice, she called, "Kaldi Willensson!"

Rhianna's mind seemed somehow to race, and somehow to freeze, both at the same time. The Wisewoman — Merched, Eriseth had named her — shook her head, amused, appearing regretful. "Kaldi is a little out of place here, in our forests. I had to leave him at the bottom of the slope. Even you, Eriseth, would have heard him coming."

A minute passed, and then a man came into sight, moving heavily up the slope. He was a big man, red-bearded and strong. Rhianna recognized him, and at the same instant she heard Eriseth's gasp. The sea captain from the ship in port.

He came into the stone clearing, moved to the top of its low height, and frowned down at them, taller than any of them by head and shoulders and more, massive and bulky besides. "So this is the Wild Mage?" he growled. "Hah! We almost had her before this, and did not know it."

Rhianna had then an inkling of what Merched intended. She looked at Gorsayd, the Eldra hunter. "You've been with us for more than a week, you said. So you were there when Magister Northstar — Serenir — was speaking of bespelling iron, weren't you? Sneaking and prying under our windows, most likely."

Gorsayd stood unsmiling. "I did as my Wisewoman bid," she replied.

Merched turned to the redbearded man. "She is as I said, Kaldi. She has just confirmed it with her own mouth. And I give you Eriseth of Arwensgrove as a bonus. She is a worker in iron, and will help to make the weapons that the other will bespell. They are yours. Now I have done as I said I would."

Kaldi nodded. "King Hrothwil thanks you, and you will find that his friendship is worth having."

"I trust his friendship will be worth as much to me as the magic weapons our gift will make for him."

"More," said Kaldi, and in his voice was triumph. "It is worth far more to you. Think of the lands that Hrothwil will conquer, and the plunder he will take from their Queen. These he will share with you. You will be glad of his help when you go to war yourselves, with this Arwenna. And then the Easterners will be in no shape to resist you when you carry your war to them, afterwards, and thrust them from this island."

The final pieces of the puzzle clicked into place. "You would ally with the Western Islanders?" Rhianna asked. "They've raided your coasts, and ours, since time beyond telling."

Eriseth nodded, and continued the thought: "Aye, and you would ally with them against your own people, what's more. You are a traitor as well as a fool, Merched Simpleton. Do you really think that the Western Islanders will spare the Eldra when they have their weapons of be-spelled steel?"

Merched said nothing, but her eyes flicked to Kaldi. Eriseth followed the glance, and nodded her head in un-derstanding. "Or perhaps you have an agreement that the Western Islanders will give you such weapons as well. I do not think even you are such a fool as to believe that. But, you think, at least they will be fighting Rhianna's people, and so both the nations of the Clumsy Ones will be at war, allowing you to have a war of your own. Against your own folk." Eriseth nodded at Gorsayd, who stood staring at the Wisewoman. "And have you told your own followers of this plan, Merched the False?"

Kaldi reached out. He held a length of hard cord. "I have no time for chatter. My ship lies at the mouth of this river, and sooner or later one of the Queen's ships will happen past and people will start asking questions. Now, listen. I will bind you, and you will walk."

Rhianna and Eriseth looked at each other, and then Rhianna spoke. "I'll never make magic for the likes of you," she spat.

But the Westerner only grinned. "Aye? It's surprising

what folk will do when they haven't eaten or drunk for a few days, or maybe someone's tickling their feet with a hot iron. We've experience with that sort of thing, we have. I don't think we'll have too much trouble with you, lass. Now put your hands behind your back. Or I break your arms before I tie them." He tied their hands, hard, with a seaman's skill, and then joined the bindings with a cord the length of his arms, so that they could not separate from each other.

"Now," he grunted when he had done. "Back to the *Raven*." He measured the shadows with his eye. "The sun will set in an hour. We must be there by then. That will give us the night and a tide to slip past any Queen's ships that might be about."

Merched smiled. "We'll be going, then. I shall be sure to tell the Council of the Wisewomen that one of our very own people — Eriseth Arwensgrove, poor lass — has been kidnapped by the Clumsy Ones and carried off as a slave. I always said we could never trust them." She glanced at the two girls, alike in their rain-cloaks, both silent and staring down at the stone and leaf-litter. "Unless you think you'll need our help with them, Kaldi?"

The sea rover laughed. "With these? A jest! And I can find my way all right. All I need to do is follow the river."

"Don't forget, one of them has the Wild Magic."

"Much use it will be to her. The first hint of a fog or a bogle, and it'll be this across her shoulders." He pulled off his belt, a length of tough, supple steerhide. It made a singing sound as he swung it, and Rhianna shrank away. He laughed again. "Never had the strap taken to you, missy? Well, mind your manners, and it won't be. But mind them well, now. And the same for your friend."

"Farewell, then," said Merched, and the two Eldra receded into the trees.

Kaldi watched them go. Then he twitched on the rope. "Come along," he said.

It was the worst hour of Rhianna's life. She was already tired, but that was the least of it. The Wild Magic was low, too, and it took time to build it again. But what good would it do if she did build it up? The sea rover trod behind her, never taking his eyes off her. They angled back towards the river, following a trail of sorts along its bank. The river would lead them towards the sea. There was no escape.

Rhianna knew that all the worst of Magister Northstar's fears were realized. The Wild Magic had been loosed on the world, and along with that went bespelled steel and whatever monsters she could be made to summon. But that was nothing, nothing at all, beside Father, sickening gradually, weakening, fading and . . . dying.

And she couldn't help. It was all her fault, and she couldn't help.

She could say nothing to Eriseth. Wrapped in her sorrow, she wept, helplessly and uselessly, for it made no difference at all. But Eriseth wept with her.

CHAPTER 8

In the red of the sunset the river opened out. The further bank receded. By slow degrees the river became a funnel-shaped inlet. In the long wedge of water, where the fresh met the salt, a ship rocked at anchor beyond the river-bar.

They came down to a shelving narrow beach, where small waves curled and smacked against pebbles.

Kaldi grunted with satisfaction. "Time to stop your carrying on now, lass. Buck up. You'll be living in a palace this time next week." Rhianna said nothing. Tears dripped off her chin, and she couldn't wipe them away.

Kaldi grinned, then filled his lungs. "Ahoy!" he shouted, cupping his hands towards the ship.

Nothing but echoes answered him. He waited while they died away, then shook his head. "Useless set of scrobies," he muttered. "I told them to keep a watch. If they've all gone for a swim in the ale-cask, I'll . . . Here. This way."

He turned them to the right, and walked a few more paces along the beach. A dinghy was pulled up there, above the high-water mark, its oars racked neatly inside it.

"One either side," he said. "Here, and here. The rope will reach between you, don't worry. Grab the gunwale. The top plank. We'll run her down into the water." He positioned himself at the bow. The stern was closest to the water's edge. "Ready? Heave!"

Rhianna made as little effort as possible, and Eriseth undoubtedly did the same, but Kaldi was strong enough for all three of them. The boat crunched across the pebbles and into the water, where it floated free.

Kaldi held the rope. "Ladies first. In you get. Into the sternsheets, where I can watch you. The bench at the back. Go on. And remember, those as can't use their hands can't swim, either." He pushed off and boarded in the same motion, neat and quick, and had the oars out in a moment. He turned the boat and pulled towards the ship, watching them, checking his direction in quick glances over his shoulder.

The boat kissed up against the ship's side. It was low in the middle, low enough for them to climb over the rail. Kaldi urged them up with a shove from underneath, and then sprang up himself and tied the boat up.

The *Raven* was a single-masted Western Isles trader, wide and deep. Her cargo was carried in bales and barrels, packed low, lashed down. At the very bottom was a layer of iron billets, used both for ballast and trade goods. Over the top of the cargo a plank gangway had been laid, and the crew used that to get from fore to aft, from the foresails to the rudder. The sails were furled, and there was no movement on the deck.

Kaldi took a long stride from the side to the gangway, and hauled his captives across with a pull on the rope that connected them. When they cried out, he snarled at them. "Shut, or I give you reason to yell." He gazed around, hard eyes probing the shadows. Then his chest expanded, and he called, "Leifar! Torsen! Where are you?" No answer. "Regnal! You . . . hey!"

Rhianna stood on the gangway, head lowered. She had no interest in this. Perhaps Kaldi's crew had deserted. That would be too good to be true, for surely he could not sail all the way to the Western Isles on his own. Then she raised her head and saw the direction he was looking. She followed his eyes to a box of some sort, a large one, with a tarpaulin over it. The tarpaulin had been lashed down with ropes, but some of them had parted, and it had fallen partly to the side. Lying in the shadow between the box and the keel of the ship was a crooked object. Squinting at it, Rhianna realized that it was a man's foot.

Kaldi leaped down, and as his feet touched the hull, his sword flashed out. He looked at the foot, then at the rest of the man, still out of sight to Rhianna and Eriseth, and even his hard face twitched. Then he pulled at the tarpaulin.

It fell to the deck, over the man who still lay there. The box was revealed. It was no box, but a cage, low so that a man would have to crouch to go within, but made of iron bars.

"A slaver's cage," hissed Eriseth, and Kaldi flicked a glance at her.

"Every Western Islander has one, lass. They come in useful. Now keep silence. There's more here than I care for."

Rhianna stared. Within the cage was a set of chains. She couldn't be sure, for the light was starting to fail, but she could see a broken link, and on that broken link . . .

"Look, Eris," she breathed, low, too low for Kaldi's ears. "On the link that lies on the floor of the cage. Can you see?"

Eriseth looked, and her eyes narrowed. "You have good eyes, Rhianna. That link has been—"

"Chewed. By something that has a mouth like a file. A mouth full of iron teeth."

Kaldi stooped under the gangway and went forward, and for a few seconds they lost sight of him. Then he suddenly sprang out of the cargo-well on the far side of the gangway, hauled himself up, and strode to the afterdeck. The tiller was untended, and swung idly.

Bending, Kaldi looked carefully at the deck. His sword was still in his hand.

There was a rattle forward, where the foredeck met the gangway. A bale of wool was lashed there, wrapped in hessian. There was a ripping, puncturing sound, as if a man were digging a baling hook into the hessian, ready to unload it, but doing that time after time after time. And then . . .

A rust-red head appeared above the bale. No, not rust-red all over. The jaws were splashed with brighter, sharper red, red that dripped. Rhianna shrank inside when she realized what it was. The head was lean and sharp, and Eriseth gasped to recognize her own work and that of her Master. For it was indeed the other dog. Its red-brown body appeared, it reached the foredeck, and there it stopped and grinned at them, hunching a little to ease its shoulders.

For an instant they stood thus, the dog on the fore-deck, Kaldi on the afterdeck, and Rhianna and Eriseth in between, standing on the narrow gangway. And then the dog started towards them.

It walked slowly, as if its knees hurt. Eriseth drew in breath, head bowed, prepared to accept what would come. But Rhianna gestured backwards with her bound hands. She had watched the dog, and she had seen where its eyes were fixed. She stepped back, and perforce Eriseth stepped back also, both of them onto a bundle of sweetcane. They slid down it until they reached the ship's bottom, leaving the gangway free for the dog.

It stalked forward, not taking any notice of them. It didn't seem interested in them. After all, they had not captured it. They had not shut it in a cage, nor clamped a chain to its leg, nor wet it with salt water that made it rust. Its red little eyes were locked on Kaldi, who had done those things.

Rhianna and Eriseth watched as it passed them, its iron paws clicking and scraping on the planking. Its teeth were still sharp and bright, but the rest of it was rusting, red-rotten with corrosion. It walked, not quite limping, but slowly and painfully; and its eyes were glowing bright.

Kaldi straightened and watched it come. For a moment perhaps he might have thought to fling himself overboard. But his face stiffened, and he spoke to the dog as it stalked towards him.

"I am Kaldi, son of Willen, son of Thorsten, son of Svart, son of Guthlad, who came from Theunissland and slew the bear. I am of the blood of Tostig Red-hand, Burner of Ships, and there is no dog, iron or flesh, that shall drive me from my own deck. Come! We shall try our steel together." He laughed, throwing his head back, and as he did so, the dog snarled like a saw-blade and broke into a run.

It was a clumsy run, heavy, slow, and yet it had power and weight. It doubled its body, hindquarters pumping, and its steel claws dug grooves in the planking as it strove to accelerate. Kaldi still laughed, and Rhianna realized it was a feint, for then his head snapped forward again. His sword was out in his hand, and he swung as the dog sprang at his throat.

Steel blade met iron body in midair with a shower of sparks and rust. Kaldi's eye was true and the stroke was measured, and he had struck with all the strength of arm and back and loins. Yet still all he did was knock it aside, and notch his blade. The dog clanged to the deck, scrabbling to get its feet under it, and the sword whirled up again, an overhand stroke aimed at its neck.

Kaldi was a strong man, and the sword was a fine one. He stepped forward as he struck, putting all his weight into the blow. The steel bit into the iron body, and a cloud of rust went up. Even so, Loys Wildwood had forged that iron, and he had forged it well. It was notched, but the thinner sword blade was hurt worse. There was a rending metal crack, and the blade broke across. Steel splinters tinkled on the deck. Kaldi stared at the broken stub in his hand, and then the dog leaped again for his throat.

Its weight knocked him over, big as he was. They rolled on the deck together, red-iron dog and red-haired man, worrying and struggling, and Rhianna knew that she had to stop it. It had to be stopped. This was not right. No matter what Kaldi had done, to allow this would be to act like him, or worse. But there was only one way to stop it.

She called on the Wild Magic, drawing on the fire-magic of the weak sun, on the salt of the sea, and the dissolving power of water. The rust flowed as fast as the running waves over the body of the dog, quickly, quickly. It stiffened, corrosion biting into it even as it was biting Kaldi. Rhianna twisted at her bonds, but they were tight and not to be broken. All the power of her magic she was using on the dog.

Eriseth had backed herself against the gangway and was fraying the cord around her wrists against the corner of a plank, but that would take far too long for any good it might do. Rhianna called harder, and the Wild Magic answered.

Kaldi wrenched himself upright, and tore the dog from him. He hurled it to the deck, and it shattered like a flung pot, rust-red shards exploding across the planking. Staggering, he kicked at a piece. It skittered over the deck, through the rail, and into the water.

He raised his face to the sky. Blood poured from his wounds. "Hear me!" he called, and his voice was strong and glad. "I am Kaldi, son of Willen, of the blood of Tostig Ship-burner, and I have killed the iron dog! Let the deed be . . . let it be . . . remembered . . . in the sagas . . ." He raised the broken stub of his sword to the sky, and then he pitched forward on his face and died.

CHAPTER 9

Part of the *Raven*'s cargo was oil in barrels from Githra, far to the south. When Eriseth had finally worn through her bonds and released Rhianna in her turn, they broke in the heads of a few oil-casks and scattered the oil around. They splashed it on deck and sails, on tarred ropes, and canvas-wrapped cargo.

Rhianna went to the afterdeck and straightened the limbs of Kaldi, son of Willen. She left his broken sword in his hand, but took his seaman's knife. She closed his eyes. Then she tied the tiller, so that the ship would steer straight before the offshore wind.

She stood for a moment, then she turned and walked up the gangway. In the bows, she cut the anchor-rope. Eriseth had laid out tinder, flint, and steel. She struck a spark, expert here as in the forest, and blew the tinder to life.

Rhianna used the knife to peel shavings off a deck

plank. Then she pried up some of the decking, which was only pegged down. The flames were already rising. She fed them with the pieces.

Eriseth looked up, a question in her eyes. Rhianna nodded. She picked up the bag of ship's rations they had found. They stepped over the side, and down into the dinghy, taking an oar each, and cast off. A few strokes took them clear, and they rowed steadily back to the beach, watching the flicker of the spreading flames.

Ashore, they stood and watched in the gathering darkness, saying nothing. The wind and the tide took the *Raven* out. They watched as the flames leaped higher and the ship moved steadily out to sea, carrying its cargo. It passed between the headlands, becoming a flare on the water, then a flicker.

When it was a glow on the horizon, they turned and moved into the trees of the land of the Eldra. They camped there, for both of them were weary, but they stayed only long enough to eat and sleep a few hours. Long before dawn they were moving again.

Eriseth went with Rhianna as far as the ford to make sure she was on the right road, and then they parted. Eriseth took the trail that led further into the deep woods towards Arwensgrove. Rhianna reached into her pocket and put on her jewel, snuffing out the Wild Magic once more. Then she set her face towards her home.

It was still early in the morning when she passed beyond the trees and started down the slope to the fields of Smallhaven. The weather was clearing; cold, but the sun rose among light clouds, seeming stronger than even a week before. Spring had come.

Rhianna lengthened her stride. She was almost running by the time she came in sight of her home.

The Council of the Wisewomen of the Eldra met at the dark of the moon in the center of a grove that crowned a rounded hill. Here there were no houses, not even the green walls that the Eldra built around their home-trees. There were only the trees themselves, massive and ancient beyond reckoning, and in their midst a clearing in the stony soil at the hill's peak. It was large enough for forty or so to sit in a circle around a fire, none of them above any of the others.

The fire had burned low, for the debate had gone on for hours.

"What more proof do you need, Arwenna?" asked Merched, her voice carrying easily across the circle. "What measure shall you put to their treachery now? You sent them one of our own, a fine young hunter. They could hardly refuse you, so good a friend have you been to them — and so they took her." She looked about in the firelight. "Yes, took her. Perhaps they thought, *This one is Eldra, and will not learn the craft of iron.* And perhaps that was right, or should have been, for iron is no craft for the Eldra. Yet she learned it, and learned it too well, poor lass. They saw that and were jealous, and in their malice they sold her to their brothers from the Western Isles."

The eyes of the Wisewomen watched her, reflecting the fire glow, frowning, sad, worried, or sparking with anger. Arwenna alone watched the others and felt the balance of their thoughts tottering, and the work of thirty years tottering with it.

"How can you read their minds and speak of jealousy and malice, Merched?" she asked as Merched paused, sensing the same thing. "I think those feelings are well known to you, so well known that you see them in others, even when they are not there."

Merched's lip curled. "Then how do you explain it, Arwenna *Wisewoman?* She was of your Grove, and she trusted you, and now she is a **slave in** Westoway. Such a thing would *shame* me, if I were **her W**isewoman. If I had not sent one of my own to watch, we would not know even so much as that. The Clumsy Ones would be able to spread their hands and shrug and say they do not know where she went. They would lie to us, Arwenna the Wise. They would lie, as they have lied to you all along. But now we can throw their lies in their teeth." She flung her arms out and faced around. "And if we would not all be like that unfortunate girl, slaves in Westoway or Avalon, we *must* throw their lies in their teeth. Aye, and follow the lies with the arrow's point. For Eriseth trusted the Clumsy Ones, as she trusted Arwenna, and now . . ."

She spoke on, and as she spoke a runner slipped up behind Arwenna and whispered in her ear. Arwenna frowned, and then her face cleared. It almost seemed as though she would break into a shout, but then her mask dropped into place, and she nodded. The other slid away into the darkness beyond the firelight.

Arwenna waited a moment, and then rose.

Merched turned on her. "I have not finished speaking, Arwenna. No doubt you think you can set the rule of the Council at naught, as you have set at naught every other part of the life of the Eldra, but the rule is that a speaker is heard —"

"— until the Council decides not to hear her further. Yes. And if the Council wishes to hear you further after it has seen this, then let it. You speak of throwing lies into faces, Merched. Here is one to do it for you."

She turned and beckoned. Eriseth of Arwensgrove stepped into the ring of firelight. Arwenna stood behind her, taller, darker of hair, but with the same face, the same eyes. It was as if one person stood and smiled at Merched the Wise.

Merched stared at them, and her mouth opened, but nothing came out.

With warmth Eriseth remembered that Council as she looked down the slope to the fields of Smallhaven. Those fields were bare no longer. There was a haze of green over them, and the fresh scent of the turned ground was as fine as the forest's own scents, in its way. That had been a fine night. She hoped — oh, how she hoped — that this would be as fine a day.

She wondered if indeed Merched — who was called the Wise no longer — could have been a little bit right. In every good lie there is a little truth, and Merched the Traitor was a good liar. Could Eriseth, who had gone to learn the craft of the Clumsy Ones, be more like them than she was Eldra?

Perhaps. Eriseth left the thought and the shelter of the trees behind without a backward glance, and hurried down the slope. Remembering Merched's downfall was a comfort in a way, but it did nothing to allay Eriseth's other fears.

She broke into a run when she came in sight of the house. The windows were open to the sunshine and the breeze, and that might mean anything or nothing. She left her bow leaning on the step, and had the door open before it passed through her mind to call out or knock.

Meg Wildwood stood at the kitchen table, kneading bread. She looked around as Eriseth came in, and brought her floury hands out of the dough. She smiled a little, and dusted them off. Eriseth stood in the doorway, unable to speak.

"You need not look for your Master here, Eriseth," said Meg. She sighed. "It's a working day. He's at his forge, pounding on his iron. And missing his apprentice."

The breath gusted out of Eriseth in a *whoop*, as if she had just laid down a heavy weight. She straightened, almost staggering, and then the joy came leaping up into her throat, threatening to burst out and swamp her.

Meg Wildwood stepped around her table and opened her arms, floury to the elbow as they were, and Eriseth Arwensgrove came into them as if coming home at last.

Magister Northstar walked with Rhianna down to the harbor in the mild spring sunshine, his staff clicking on the cobbles every other stride. There was a ship at the pier, ready to sail for Avalon.

He spoke to his apprentice. "Old as I am, I am still learning about magic, Rhianna — the Wild Magic most of all. I still don't know how you bespelled iron. That was unheard of. I hope it remains unheard of. The secret is safe for now, I think. Kaldi and his crew knew, but they are dead, and as for Merched and Gorsayd, who would believe them now, whatever they say? None among the Eldra, and I think that they will have trouble getting any sort of hearing from King Hrothwil. He dislikes those who promise much and deliver nothing. Not that they will be able to ask him, for they will be watched every day they live, stripped of rank and disgraced as they are."

He frowned, and continued. "All the same, rumor may get out. We will listen for it, and at the first hint of trouble, I think you had better come to Avalon and Wizardly College. I hope it won't be for some time, but you would have to come and study anyway, some day. And teach. We have to learn about this bespelling of iron before others do."

Rhianna nodded.

He sighed. "And yet, the worst of it wasn't that the dogs were made of iron. They were far more dangerous than that. I think I was right about the poison in their bite." He considered. "Remember? Jealousy, envy, ignorance, neglect, anger. Those are fit to poison anything, and the dogs were made of those things, not iron alone. That's why I don't think it was their destruction that cured your father."

"Master? But it happened at the very same moment. Soon after sunset that very night, you said, he rallied, and the wound dried up. The poison was drawn."

They passed the smithy, where Loys Wildwood was

sizing a horseshoe. Eriseth, frowning in concentration, was rasping at the hoof, the horse's forefoot turned up between her knees, to get the seat for it right.

Rhianna and her Master waved, but the pair were busy, and could only look up and wave back briefly. Rhianna had seen them at breakfast, and would again at dinner. They would be full of cheerful talk about their work, yet listening to her when she spoke of the Wild Magic, and to Mother singing in the kitchen. She wondered briefly how it could be that her father could acquire an apprentice, Mother another daughter, she herself a sister, and Eriseth a family, all in one go. It had so nearly all been lost forever. Then she shrugged. Magic. The Wild Magic, perhaps.

Magister Northstar returned to the subject. "Yes, but was the cure caused by the dogs' destruction? I don't think so. Destruction would only be a worse poison." They strolled on, slowly. "No," he said. "I think it was this: to the dogs, you returned pity and mercy, and the acceptance of responsibility; to Kaldi, you returned honor for his courage, and decency in his dying, despite his wrongdoing. Pity, mercy, responsibility, charity, honor, decency. The very things that would draw those poisons. Perhaps it was that."

"And to Merched and Gorsayd the Shadow?" asked Rhianna. "What is returned to them?"

A grim smile curved the wizard's mouth. "Why, the best returns of all. Truth for their lies, justice for their wrong, and goodwill for their malice." He nodded. "Goodwill, indeed. The Council of Wisewomen has said that they will speak to our Queen's Council about an alliance between us, and send others to learn the craft of iron. Eriseth will be the first, though. Arwenna . . . sent to say that she will be watching her progress with great care. And that she is glad that Eriseth is happy with me. Among us, that is."

He hesitated, and seemed as if he would say more, but then shook his head and fell silent. They walked on towards the ship that would take him across the sea again. Birds flew overhead, heading north and west to where the ice was melting in the Western Isles.

ABOUT THE AUTHOR

DAVE LUCKETT writes in many genres, but his first loves are fantasy and science fiction. He has won many accolades for his work, including three Aurealis Awards.

Although he was born in New South Wales, Dave has lived most of his life in Perth, Western Australia. A full-time writer, he is married with one son.

When Magic Is Too Powerful, It Can Get Wild

The Girl, the Dragon, and the Wild Magic

Dave Luckett

Rhianna is failing out of magic school. She's rather clumsy, even though she tries her best. After she causes her biggest mess ever, a wizard appears with some astonishing news — Rhianna's magic is, in fact, stronger than anyone else's. She's a Wild Talent, which means that she possesses a pure form of magic that is full of power and energy. The hitch? Well, it's very hard to control wild magic. And it tends to suck up all the other magic around it. So when a dragon comes to town, it's up to Rhianna to save the day.

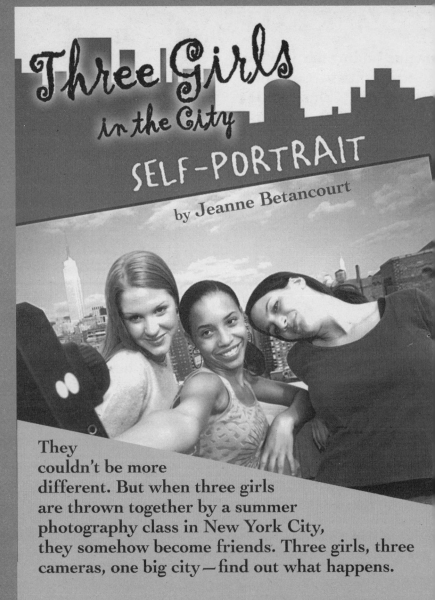